A Tear for Memory

By
Kathryn Lynn Davis

Duncurra LLC

www.duncurra.com

Copyright 2014 by Kathryn Lynn Davis

ISBN-10:1-942623-34-8

ISBN-13:978-1-942623-34-2

Cover Art by Earthly Charms

Produced in the USA

Prologue

A babe lay breathing raggedly in the aftermath of the Forty-Five—of the slaughter at Culloden Moor, when Scotland lost her Prince, her pride, her honor and her heritage to the British, to the Duke known as The Butcher.

But the babe's birthright was neither of one side nor the other, and her mother's blood, like her tears, sprayed white blankets red and stained her pale and hollow cheek. For a time, like the land in which she had been born, the babe was ruined, vulnerable, defenseless.

It rained that day in fear and mourning, weeping from the dark and heavy skies to wash away the blood of the thousand dead—and the tears of those still living. That rain turned to a rising wind and took wing, blowing with a ferocity unknown before or since.

It blew so high and piercing that it reached the Ancient Ones, the Wise Ones who treasured their magic and their gifts in a secret cave, hidden from the eyes and yearning and violence of mankind.

Until it reached and circled Dearshul and she raised her head; within the wind, she heard the babe's weak cry. Dearshul was called True Eye—she who sees all truth—be it good or dreadful, bring it hope or fear to the human heart.

But she was not alone.

For the wail of the fierce and searching wind reached also the kind, broken heart of the babe's aunt, Clare, and the two came together—Dearshul and Clare—to save the babe from her mother's fate.

Her aunt wished upon the tiny baby ignorance of the turmoil and pain that had created her; and so, with a tear, Clare named her Caelia, which means blind.

A Tear for Memory

The Wise One blessed the babe with The Sight, so she would see clearly; so she would know the truth of what had been and what would come to be.

And both things came to pass.

But not as either had expected or foreseen.

Chapter 1

The day Caelia Rose finally began to sketch her first self-portrait was also the day when Robert Hamilton appeared at Fairies' Haven. And one had nothing to do with the other.

Or so she told herself.

The storm from the night before had worn itself out, and the piercing wail of the wind had shrunk to a whisper of breeze that morning. Caelia felt exhilarated by the memory of the furious rain: windborn and exciting. She had always loved wild storms. Her Aunt Clare found that unsettling; it went against everything else in her niece's calm, contented nature. Caelia didn't care why she was so enthralled, why she so yearned to answer the voice of the tears in the wind. She simply reveled in the many storms that passed through Glen Affric and over Fairies' Haven— the name the people of the glen called her home.

Caelia had left the manor house early, wearing the red Rose plaid and carrying a special leather case containing blending brushes, pastels, cloths and her portfolio, with her low easel and blank canvas under the other arm. She loved to catch the morning light, especially after a storm, when it took on a shimmering, newly washed quality. She wanted to seize it before it faded into the late morning when the dew was absorbed by the sun.

She looked about as she went, soaking in the drenched greens of the pines, birches and oaks, and the verdant ferns along her path. Smiling, she began to whistle softly. "Tis a beautiful day, is't no', Davy?" she said to a tow-headed boy approaching her with his brightly painted wagon.

The skinny lad, all elbows and knees, came forward with his fancifully designed wooden wagon. "Aye, Miss

3

Caelia." He blushed more than usual at the attention, but did not want to tell her why. She might stop smiling and he didn't want that.

"Are ye all right? Ye look a bit warm." As always, Celia was concerned. She bent down to meet him at his own level.

"I'm no' ill again, if that's what ye mean. No' since ye painted the pitcher wi' the shadow on my eyes. Tis all gone now."

"Are ye sure? Are ye seein' clearly again?"

Davy wiggled as she looked into his clear green eyes, then glanced at the wagon. "Aye, so I am! Jest look what I found, Miss Caelia, look!"

A smattering of stones lay in the bottom of the wagon: green ones, red, pink, blue ones and some sparkly silver ones. He had been in burn beds picking out the smooth colored stones to match colors she had painted on his wagon when his eyesight failed because of an illness. The shadow had appeared in her portrait of the boy—as things sometimes did, though she could not explain why. Her friends called it a gift, but it made Caelia uneasy, in spite of the gratitude she felt when these strange things helped someone like Davy. She had told the healer about the shadow, and old Morven had given the boy special herbs to treat his eyes. He was blind for a short while, and then he could see hazy shapes and brightness. That was when Caelia painted the wagon so he'd be able to spot it easily. Now he could see well enough to find the light stones.

She grinned and hugged him. "They're aye very bonnie, Davy. Bonnie as yer cheeks from the chill of mornin'."

He wriggled out of her grasp, blushing furiously. She was his friend; she always smiled at him. And look how he had betrayed her. "I'm sorry."

He was so bereft she wanted to pull him into her arms and hold him all day. "Ye've nothin' to be sorry for, my friend. Nothin' at all."

He could hold it in no longer. "Nay, but I do. I was indestreet. Mam says I shouldna, but I canna help it sometimes."

She had no idea what he was talking about, but she sensed how important it was to him. To laugh it off would distress him. "Weel," she rubbed her heart-shaped chin between thumb and forefinger, "since ye've said sorry, I forgive ye here and now, and that's an end on it."

He frowned at her doubtfully.

"Will ye shake on it?" she asked. "If ye don't, twill break my heart."

Davy could never do that. Never. "Aye then, I will."

They shook hands solemnly, then he grinned and wheeled his little wooden wagon away. Caelia heard him whistling as he disappeared down the brae.

She continued on her way, yearning to run her fingers through the celandine, the bluebells and starflowers, but her hands were full. Still, she soaked in the color and beauty of the spring flowers until she found her favorite spot by the loch, where she was fond of sitting when she painted. She set her gear down with great care, then tip-toed over the cotton grass, noticing the delicate web of rain and dewdrops lying like gossamer gems beneath the confusion of emerald blades. The sun shone across it, making the woven web gleam.

Climbing the few rocks up into a cave she used to store the other things she needed, she found the heavy horse blanket and low-cushioned chair the carpenter had fashioned for her so she would be comfortable while she sat and painted. She returned to lay the thick blanket—folded over and over again—on her favorite rock, then placed the chair just so. Growing excited at her ambitious project, she opened her case to remove her pastels and a mirror. The mirror was less shiny than she would like, but held by a tooled silver Celtic design she loved. It had come from her mother's secret chest, and for that reason alone, she loved it. She always imagined she could see her mother, Lila Rose's face when she looked into it.

She let her plaid slip from her shoulders and, for an instant, she thought of the Jacobite rising 19 years past—the Forty-Five—when Bonnie Prince Charlie and his Highlanders tried and failed to restore James III to the British throne. The Act of Proscription afterward forbid the wearing of the plaid, along with the playing of the pipes and speaking the Gaelic language. She knew it was a risk simply to wear the tartan as a shawl. The penalties were harsh, because the British had been frightened by the rising and wanted to destroy the Highlanders' way of life—and thus their strength. But Caelia refused to fear discovery. She loved her plaid, her one link to a disappearing past she had never known, but learned of through her parents' stories and deep affection for things lost and gone.

She did not want that tragedy to cast a shadow across her painting, so she forced it down and focused on the colors and life and scents of spring all around her. She began to sing, as she was wont to do when happy and guided by her rich imagination.

How blyth this morn was I to see
The swain come o'er the hill!
He skipp'd the burn, and flew to me:
I met him with good will.

Like the river and the breeze and the waves on the loch, she created her own cadence to create to. Laying out her pastels, she reached for a skin-colored stick.

O the broom, the bonny bonny broom,
The broom of Cowdenknows:
I wish I were with my dear swain,
With his pipe and my ewes.

Kathryn Lynn Davis

Glancing from the mirror to the canvas, she began with the line from the top of her head to her chin.

He did oblige me every hour,
Could I but faithful be?
He stole my heart:
Could I refuse
Whate'er he ask'd of me?

Soon she was lost in the rhythm and pulse of music and color as she swept her hand over the canvas in arcs of vivid hue. She propped the mirror on a rock so the ferns crept around the edges, blending with the image of her long, light brown hair. Hair and ferns and grasses met and melded, danced and rippled in mirror and earth, as shades of emerald, verdant jade and olive blended with bronze, clear tea, and chestnut in an a bewitching pattern.

O the broom, the bonny bonny broom,
The broom of Cowdenknows:
I wish I were with my dear swain,
With his pipe and my ewes.

~ * ~

Hidden among the trees, Robert Hamilton observed the young woman with great interest. He did not know what he had expected, but it hadn't been this. She was lovely and serene, with her high curved cheekbones tinted pink from the sun. She obviously spent a lot of time outdoors; her smooth skin, which would have otherwise been pale, was sun-kissed a light tan. She moved gracefully, intently, mesmerizing him as she touched chalk to canvas. Mesmerizing herself, he guessed, from the faraway look in her golden-brown eyes.

As he watched, he forgot, for nearly half an hour, why he had come. He could see her innocence in her eyes, her graceful movements, her secret smiles into the distance.

Her light brown hair hung long and loose, like a young girl's, and her beauty was soft-spoken, gentle, untouched by darkness or misery.

When or if he fulfilled his mission—he wondered again why he had agreed to it at all—he feared he would damage that innocence and untouched beauty.

Then go, he told himself silently. *Turn right now and go away.*

Glowering at the rich, dark loam of the forest floor, he ran his fingers through his thick brown hair. "I can no' turn away," he murmured. He was caught. Already and without a word.

~ * ~

Caelia kept rhythm with the pulse of the loch caressing the tinted stones on the shore. Her voice mingled with the soft song of the water, casting a spell over the day.

Adieu, ye Cowdenknows, adieu,
Farewell all pleasures there;
Ye gods, restore me to my swain,
Is all I crave or care.

She sketched from instinct, letting her fingers go where they would. She was never happier than when she was painting with her pastels. When she finally paused to look at what she had drawn, she sighed. It was lovely, like a portrait of a mermaid in the grass that was its own sea—but it did not look like her.

She had tried simply sketching her face several times, but she could never get it right. She always got distracted by other beautiful things that worked their way in where they didn't belong. But since her nineteenth birthday last week, she was certain she had become a lady, mature enough, not only to sketch her self-portrait, but also to paint it with her cherished pastels. Brow furrowed, she opened her portfolio case.

Chapter 2

Caelia froze. Inexplicably, she was certain she was being watched. She turned, two-sided blending tool in hand like a miniature claymore. After the Forty-Five, the Butcher had passed a law forcing the Highlanders to give up their weapons, especially the deadly, two-edged claymore. *Why're ye so obsessed with the uprising the day?* she wondered.

"Who is't?" she called out.

Silence, heavy and ominous, filled the air.

Caelia's eyes never wavered from a spot between the trees at the edge of the forest where the shade was deep. "Stop hidin'!" she demanded, surprised by the severity of her tone. She was usually quite soft-spoken.

For one more moment stillness fraught with motion hung in the air, and then a stranger stepped from the protection of the trees.

Just an ordinary gentleman, she told herself. And a well-dressed one at that. He didn't look threatening, and her fear dissipated. She smiled to make up for having spoken harshly. "Hello," she said, unobtrusively studying his smart breeches and waistcoat.

"Hello, Caelia Rose. Tis a lovely day, is't no'?" His tipped his tricorn hat to her, observing her casually draped plaid with interest.

Pulling it over her shoulders to show she was proud of the red tartan, she asked him coolly, "Who are ye and how do ye know my name?"

The man seemed taken aback, as if he had not expected the question. Or perhaps he did not wish to reply. "I heard it in the village, lass. They speak of ye often and fondly. And if ye don't know my name, then I'll tell ye, though tis no' a formal introduction. Tis Robert Hamilton." He inclined his head in lieu of a bow, hazel eyes watching her intently.

Caelia was not particular about formal introductions, though her father and aunt had tried again and again to impress their importance upon her. She trusted her instincts. What unsettled her was that he had been talking to people about her when he was a complete stranger. She shifted nervously.

It struck him then why he had not been able to make himself leave; he would have stopped regardless of his errand, Robert realized. She made a charming picture, poised as she was with her feet curled beneath her, her long hair flowing loose down the back of her flattering blue gown, pooling in the ends of the red plaid. She'd been concentrating on the drawing on her easel, lips pursed in displeasure.

Attempting to turn her attention back to her sketch, Caelia made a line with her chalk that rather resembled a snake.

"Don't ye want to know what they say about ye?" Robert asked with a crooked smile.

"We're friends, most all of us. Tis all I need to know." She smiled again—a calm, unruffled smile.

For some reason it irritated him. "So ye have no enemies, young Caelia?"

She furrowed her sun-touched brow in thought and glanced at him without guile. "I don't think so." Shaking her head so her hair danced, she added, "Or if I do, they've stayed away and told me naught about it, so that's all right."

Her eyes were clear, unclouded by suspicion.

Robert Hamilton became more irritated still. He began to think she might be a fool—plaid and all. There were many proud Highlanders who yearned to return to the world they'd known before the Act of Proscription in 1746, but none who ignored the law so nonchalantly. "They say ye're a Healer, do the people in the town."

"No," she said, "I am not that." She saw he was waiting expectantly. "Tis only that I paint my friends' portraits," she waved her hand toward the portfolio, "and things appear—"

He took her gesture as an invitation. "Oh, aye?" He moved toward the paintings.

She held up her hand protectively. These were her prizes, her delight, her magic. He wasn't going to intrude on those things too.

"How do ye get the colors so very vivid?"

In spite of her apprehension, she could not hide her pleasure at the compliment. "Tis because of the pastels. They're nothin' but pure color with a bit of gum binder, so there's naught to diminish the hue."

"Will ye show me one, then?" For the first time his tone was soft, not quite seductive, but appealing.

She could tell he was genuinely interested, and she wanted to respond to that interest. Here in Glen Affric, most everyone knew her work. Here was an educated man—she could tell from his speech and manner—a new audience altogether. She sorted through the few canvasses and drew out a recent portrait of Mistress Boyd, the baker.

Robert Hamilton recognized her at once. He had eaten fresh bannocks and preserves for breakfast in the tiny room built out from the side of her croft for guests. They could buy baked goods, preserves, clover ale, butter and tea, and a few lucky ones could sit down at the scrubbed pine tables and read the latest broadsheets.

He was impressed by Caelia's compelling portrait of the voluptuous woman with silver-white hair sneaking out from under her mob cap. *Tis a wonderful portrait,* he thought. *She's really captured the woman's spirit. Her smile, half-hidden most of the time, her stern face softened by affection, and the generous curves of her body.*

"Her cheek's angry and swollen. She must've had a toothache that day."

"Nay, she'd not. I'd no' seen it as I went, but then, suddenly, there twas. She went to the Healer, and found twas an infection, easily treated. The Healer said if she'd come later, she would've had to pull all Mistress Boyd's teeth, and she'd have suffered all her days with mouth disease."

Caelia told the story softly and shyly. She was not bragging, but rather, discomfited by the revelations. "Tis only here so I can make her cheek look smooth and healthy again. I'd verra much like to call myself an artist, but nothin' more."

He was drawn by both by her talent and her modesty, which was honest and straightforward, an oddity among the women of his acquaintance. *But both are entirely beside the point*, he reminded himself. "Still, the stories people tell—"

She was quick to interrupt him "They only call me Healer because of what I draw. It doesn't ease them or cure them. Tis just a picture on parchment or canvas."

Her matter-of-fact, dismissive tone made him angry, especially because she was so lovely. Not a woman who would silence a room full of officers and nobles, not a Siren or a dangerous beauty, not at all like—. But no. He had promised himself he would not make comparisons. It was unreasonable, unjust even. He flicked the thought away. "Why are ye tellin' me this?" he demanded, wondering where the question had come from.

"Why are ye askin'?" she countered. "Yer questions are rather rude, considerin' I don't know ye." Caelia shut her mouth quickly. This wasn't like her at all.

With an effort, he regained control of himself. "They also call ye a Seer."

Sighing, she replied, "No, I am not that. Tis just sometimes I draw things into their portraits or my landscapes without knowin', and they think they recognize them from the past, or sometimes the future. And I let them think it, for it seems to give them comfort, even when what they see is sad."

He put his foot up on a boulder and leaned on it with his elbows. "So they call ye a Healer and a Seer, and ye call them merely fools."

She dropped her pastel and cried out. "No, I'd never— I'd no' think of them that way. They're my friends, Robert Hamilton, and ye're most certainly not!" She was genuinely upset, and though she rose and took a menacing step toward him, he did not yield.

He stared down at her portfolio. "Is your mother at home?" he asked pleasantly.

She gaped at him, affronted and unsettled by the question. "No," she said, then, "yes," then finally, "I don't know." She found it difficult to lie, even to this dark-haired nobody, who stood a good five inches taller than her 5'6". Even if she could not help but notice that every now and then, as the sunlight shifted through the clouds, it picked out a strand of mahogany among the dark brown curls. But then, she didn't care about such things. She realized he was trying to intimidate her.

He rubbed his cheek with his palm. "Here's what I make of that answer, Miss Caelia Rose. Either ye know yer mother's no' at home because ye know she's out, or because ye have no mother; or ye know she's out but think she might be back by now; or ye don't know if the woman who calls herself yer mother is, indeed, the woman who bore ye."

Her heart began to pound. "Go away!" she said fiercely, shaken by the venom in her tone. "Get ye gone or I'll get the musket!"

Caelia was shocked by her behavior, but she did not back down. She sensed a threat she did not understand and did not intend to allow.

Robert Hamilton was stunned by his own conduct. He

prided himself on always being in control. It was how he survived.

How had he let this happen? He had made a momentous mistake. He cursed under his breath, nodded shortly and, without another word, sought the dark green stillness of the woods.

Chapter 3

Though he had disappeared into the forest long since, Caelia still felt his intense hazel gaze as she closed the door and bolted it behind her.

"Ma-clare! Are ye here? Please be here."

Clare MacKinley could hear her niece all the way from the kitchen, which was far from the door she entered by. But the tone of the girl's voice made Clare drop the tart dough and go running to find her. "What is't, lass?"

She came upon her niece in the front hall, where she had dropped all her painting materials unceremoniously. Her brown-gold eyes were wide with shock, her hair windblown, and her petticoats showing beneath her rumpled blue skirt. Her cheeks were deeply flushed. Clare's heart contracted with a pain she had never thought to feel again. "What, lass?" she asked, crossing her arms tightly over her bosom.

"There was a man," Caelia sputtered.

"What do ye mean, a man?" Clare's apron and gown were dusted with flour, and some raisins had stuck where she'd splashed water.

Caelia suddenly realized how ridiculous she sounded, how ridiculous her aunt sounded—and looked. *What do ye mean, a man?* What was happening to her? A moment ago she'd been angry and afraid, and now laughter was bubbling up inside and she could not push it down again. "Ye know, of the usual sort. A head, two arms, two legs, silken stockin's for his fancy buckled shoes. I'm no' sure what the russet breeches were made of, but they looked aye lovely to the touch. And then there was the silk embroidered waistcoat—very fine work, it seemed to me. Frock coat of superior wool. A strong man, muscular arms and legs, and rather handsome as well. Hazel eyes and curly dark brown hair." She said this last longingly, then blushed when she realized what she had done. She giggled again with tears in her eyes, feeling she might fragment with the weight of conflicting emotions.

Clare attempted to take a deep breath, but the air wouldn't go down. "Exactly how long were ye with this man?"

"Five minutes at most. I barely had time to notice him."

"Really?" Clare was skeptical.

"And I was no' *with* him. He simply stopped to say 'hello'. Although he said he'd been askin' about me in the village, and he had, too." She met her aunt's eyes, then quickly looked away. "He asked the most impertinent questions."

Clare was still considering the implications of Caelia's too thorough description of the gentleman's garments. She did not wait for yet another blush to fade from her niece's cheeks. "Did he touch ye?"

"Do ye think I'd allow it and no' call for help, or stick a brush in his eye, or a charcoal? Ye taught me what to do with men like that."

Of course she had. *Ye know the goodness in our Caelia*, Clare chided herself. *She's herself and no one else.* "Caelia, my lass, twas just…I was frightened for ye and I lost my head. But tis back again where it belongs." She turned it from side to side to demonstrate. Some flour sifted from her hair to her shoulders, and from her hands to her simple dark gown.

A hint of a smile banished the concern from Celia's eyes and replaced it with tears. "I know." All at once, she threw her arms around her aunt, holding on as if her life depended on it. "I love ye, Ma-clare."

Clare MacKinley had lived the first years of her life in France with her family. They returned to Scotland when she was 12, so she had grown up speaking French. Desiring that Caelia be educated like a proper young lady, Clare had taught her to read and write French. When she was barely able to talk, she tried to call her aunt Maman, but Clare insisted the child call her by her given name. Since Celia did not really understand, she called her aunt Ma-clare and Clare had to be content with that.

"He asked about my mother. Whether she was dead, or if I even knew who she was. Why did a stranger ask me those things? Why did he talk about me in the village?"

Uncrossing her arms and sliding them around Caelia's back, Clare tried to suppress the emotions that filled her. She had managed to do that for what seemed like forever, because her niece had believed in her, always. She had been more or less happy these 19 years, hidden away at Fairies' Haven—ridiculous name that it was. Anyway, Clare didn't believe in fairies. She wished she did; she could use their help now. To protect the girl she and her brother-in-law kept strangers away when they could. But this one sounded dangerous, with his disrespectful questions. How many more did he have? There were countless perilous questions in the dusty corners of the manor house, in the cobwebs, and the light filled with dust motes filtering through the windows. In Clare and Malcolm Rose's hearts. And Celia must never hear the answers to those questions. That Clare could not allow.

Only then did her niece notice a painting turned picture to the wall. "Which one?" she asked, distracted from thoughts of the stranger.

"Graham Gordon stopped by the day. Said he keeps dreamin' of the water rushin' o'er the broken bridge and it frightens him," Clare said warily. "He asked if ye could make it look less broken."

Caelia had once made a painting of the River Affric at the point where the stone bridge crossed. As she worked, she'd been singing, lost in the music of the forest and her song. When she really looked at her work, she noticed some logs had burst violently against the bridge in the painting, knocking the huge old stones loose. Both lay in a tangle at the base, and there was something strange about the formation.

She went to bed uneasy that night and slept restlessly through a violent storm. When she rose just past dawn, the wind was still screaming, and she knew from the rain-drenched moor that the river had gone wild. She'd gotten one of the several horses remaining to her family from the stable and ridden to the Gordon croft, warning the carpenter that he had to get to the bridge and repair it without delay. When he arrived, he discovered his young daughter had gone out early to pick herbs, slipped and fallen halfway down the riverbank, where she was trapped between a rock and a log. It took Graham an hour, Caelia's horse and a good deal of pulling and shifting to free his youngest. The rain began to fall and the river rose all the while. Without Caelia's warning, the girl would surely have drowned. In the end she had a good many scratches and bruises, as well as a bad sprain, but no broken bones.

At his request, Caelia had given him the painting. She suspected he was dreaming that he drowned, as he'd feared his daughter would. He'd wanted it as a warning, to remind him to be wary, but the warning had gone too deep. She understood without reading his brief and roughly written note that he wanted the idyllic picture of the river she had set out to create before the magic took her over.

Clare, though a strong and resourceful woman, was pale at the thought of what this piece of work meant. She didn't believe in the Sight, no matter how many times it happened. She could not explain it, so it frightened her.

Hugging her reassuringly, Caelia took the painting, facing it away from her aunt. "I'll put it upstairs," she said.

Clare would have smiled at the girl's thoughtfulness, but just then she had too much on her mind. "And Caelia,

I've asked ye before no' to wear yer plaid, but to hide it away. If anyone should see ye, ye could be fined or sent to prison."

"My friends will no' tell."

Sometimes Clare despaired over her niece's faith in others. Clare herself had learned long since never to trust anyone, especially when betrayal meant a punishment by the British who now ruled the Highlands and all of Scotland. "Mayhap no' yer friends, but what of the stranger?"

Caelia stopped still. She had not thought of that. But she remembered, in that instant, how he had stared at the red Rose plaid, as if weighing his response. He'd said nothing, but he'd certainly noticed. She shivered violently.

Chapter 4

Later, Caelia settled alone in her rooms at the top of the house, with high beamed ceilings that contrasted with the pale crean of the plaster walls. The surfaces were decorated by lush ferns, starflowers, purple foxglove and rocks covered in lichen. Near the floor, the image of a stream flowed over clear round stones, disappearing when it met the floor. Above the bed was a small green pool, reflecting blue sky and clouds overhead. Caelia smiled as she turned once to take it all in. She had made this room her haven. Even the paintings and sketches and books piled on floor and tabletop made her feel safe—lost in her own world of dreams, where no one could ever touch her.

She was going through her nightly ritual of looking over her pastel paintings, the partially filled-in pastels, finished sketches, unfinished sketches, and sketchpads. These were scattered about her bedroom and the large room next door—the studio, where she kept her canvasses and supplies.

She was always working on many pictures at a time, so she had many of each variety. Of sketchpads she had dozens, and often had trouble finding the sketch she was currently seeking: her last attempt at a drawing of her face. Today's had been a failure, but only in the sense that it did not look like her. It was a perfectly good painting of a fragile young woman, pale, with translucent skin and long shimmering bronze hair that flowed into and about the lush ferns all around her face. She looked like a fairy.

But that was Robert Hamilton's fault. She remembered his unnerving questions, pictured his handsome face, and felt uneasy all over again. She wanted to find the last sketch to compare to this, to prove that she'd done better when the mysterious stranger, who looked at her so piercingly, was absent. But she was lost among the images of her fantasies tonight, and could not locate that one slip of reality.

Lovingly, she slid her pastel sticks into their slots in the long gilt box with the fancy seal they'd come in. Her father ordered them from Paris, and he made sure she always had several boxes so she didn't run out. Sometimes she spent days or weeks trading off between her workroom and her favorite outdoor sights, painting frantically, works so many and so skilled that she could easily fill the walls of every great house in the Highlands. But she did not wish to sell them, and she was not certain why.

She always fancied she could smell a tiny whiff of honey as she slid the box closed. "No, ye silly lass, that was one of the binders ye mixed in yer watercolors before ye discovered these." She ran her fingertips over the box once more, smiling as she set the pastels on her worktable beside various knives and spoons, brushes and scrapers, and some tools that would hold fabric tight in wire frames. A pile of fabrics came next in various weights, thicknesses and textures. Near to the far wall was her turpentine, which she used rarely anymore, and her stretching materials, expensive papers, velum and canvases.

She loved the smell in this room, of old oil paint and dried watercolors, of unused linseed oil, filmed on the bottom of the bottle, of brushes and turpentine and canvasses and pigment.

She especially loved that her studio ran half the length of the wing, giving her the vaulted floor to ceiling windows filling the space from the slanted roof to the floor, which allowed the north light to pour through when she worked during the day.

Caelia found herself swaying, having gotten lost in her imagination once more. The feeling excited her and made her want to take out her chalk and sketch. But she had something else to do.

Though she had managed to smile and laugh more than once through dinner with her father and aunt, twice the laughter had quite nearly become tears. She didn't understand herself. Perhaps it was partly the falsely jovial tone Clare and her father adopted, asking casual questions about the stranger, when she knew they were worried.

"Are ye angry with me?" she'd asked. "I should no' have answered him, I ken. As soon as he called me by name, I should've turned my back and come right home."

Malcolm Rose, aged 45, with sandy hair that barely showed the grey sprinkled throughout, covered her hand with his. "We're no' angry with ye, Caelia. Just worried and somewhat curious as to whom this man might be." Like Clare, he neither powdered his hair nor wore a wig, preferring to tie it back with a leather thong. Caelia found that far more attractive than the occasional powdered, bewigged and beribboned gentlemen who passed through the glen. They inevitably made her sneeze.

"Besides," Clare interjected, "if ye'd come straight home he might have followed ye, and twould be immeasurably worse to have him on our doorstep."

"I fear twill happen by and by. Anyone can tell him where Fairies' Haven is." Caelia felt a weight in her chest, and around about it, a fluttering that confused her. Almost like anticipation. She made herself concentrate on the delicious venison cooked in cider, mace and barley, with wild leeks, carrots and garlic. Soaking up the thick gravy with oat bread, she savored the last few bites, grateful that Cook, at least, was not confused tonight.

Now, upstairs in her rooms, she unhooked her gown, untied the whalebone stays her aunt insisted she wear, slipped out of her petticoat, chemise and stockings and into her satin night rail. It slid over her warm skin like a cool caress or the kiss of a spring breeze. She closed her eyes, enjoying the feeling for a moment, then took up her silver-backed hairbrush and began to brush out her long, shining hair, working each tangle free with dexterous fingers. She could unweave as well as she wove.

When she was finished, she washed her face and hands, finishing off with her teeth; for this she used a bone with animal bristles embedded in it. And all the while a single question echoed in her head: *Is your mother at home?*

No. Her mother, Lila Rose had not been home since Caelia was born.

Here's what I make of that answer. Either ye know yer mother's no' at home because ye know she's out—

Lila Rose was often out, long before she left home for good. She'd loved her freedom, had the strikingly lovely woman with the flowing fine blonde hair.

...or because ye have no mother—Caelia had a mother, an enchantress, loved by all, but she'd been dead these 19 years since the Forty-Five. Lying in a field of strangers.

...or ye don't know if the woman who calls herself yer mother is, indeed, the woman who bore ye. Tears came to Caelia's eyes. She'd always known, from her first flicker of memory, that Clare was her aunt and not her mother. She did not need a mother; Clare worried over her, protected her, cared for her and loved her. What Caelia needed was Lila Rose—a glimpse, a moment, an afternoon with the woman who had borne her. But that could never be.

Is your mother at home? Why was that question tormenting her so? Why tonight?

But she knew why. Because Robert Hamilton—a stranger—had asked it. It came to her, as she drew a tricorn hat in the dust, as certainly as if he'd said so, that he already knew the answer. A chill sizzled from her fingertip up her arm into her heart. How did he know? And why had he asked?

It took a moment for her to realize her teeth were chattering and her body felt chilled and oddly empty. Taking a candle in hand, she went to the chest she had inherited from her mother. She had been thrilled when she was old enough to understand it was the only thing Lila had left behind, and thus it belonged to the daughter she had never known. Caelia knelt in front of it as she did on many nights, listening to the night birds beyond her window, watching the whisper of candle flame making shadows on the wall, enveloped in expectation. Every time it was the same, though she knew the contents by heart.

That first time, she had been only nine, and had lifted out the several gowns reverently, sniffing for any lingering smell or spirit of her absent mother. Any piece of precious fabric that might bring to her mind's eye, if only for an instant, her mother's form floating across the dance floor, just as she had the night Malcolm Rose proposed.

Now Caelia pushed the dresses and hats aside, along with some sketches Lila had done while a girl in Paris; she and her sister Clare had both been tutored in art and music, dance and French, English and history, so they would know everything they needed to know to catch—and hold—a husband.

There were other odds and ends: fliers from dances and concerts in Paris, dance cards from parties in Edinburgh, in Stirling Castle, at Inverary, some broadsheets about Bonnie Prince Charlie's arrival.

Caelia ignored all these things; she didn't have time for them tonight. She glanced over her shoulder out of habit, but the only sounds she heard were the whispers and groans of the huge old house of stone and ancient wood. No rustling of clothes or clicking of human feet. Carefully, quietly, she slid a board in the bottom forward, another to the left, a third to the back, and pressed. The boards lifted, revealing a small teak chest, carved at the corners with fairy wings. Carrying it carefully in one hand, balancing the candle in the other, Celia took it to the bed.

She settled herself, with the candle on the bedside table, and held the small chest close. She loved to look into its polished surface, to see the pale blur her face made on the lid. This was her secret alone. She had found it by accident one night, had known at once that it had also been Lila Rose's secret. She not want to share it with her aunt and father. It was her mother's and hers. The only thing in the world she shared only with the beautiful and mysterious Lila.

Rubbing her fingers over the carving as she always did, she marveled at the delicate lines and shapes and wondered, for the hundredth time, who had carved this exquisite chest. She opened it, peeking inside as if she'd never seen it before.

On top lay the dried yellow rose. Caelia had painted it with pine resin to preserve it, so it would not turn to dust with time. Not as her mother had. Not as Lila's relationship with her two-month-old daughter had. This, at least, would last. Holding it to her cheek, Caelia closed her eyes and wished for a dream—just a whisper of her mother's voice, the touch of her hand, the brush on her cheek of Lila's fine blonde hair, so long it fell to her knees. Next she took out the miniature painting fixed inside the lid of a pocket watch. She gazed at it curiously, though she'd memorized it long ago.

She traced her mother's wedding ring; she'd left it at Fairies' Haven the first time she went to a British Military party with her father, and never come home again.

Ignoring, for once, the letters between her aunt and her mother, Caelia thought about the other thing she had found in the box—the pastels that had changed her life. Until she discovered what they could do, that they were pure color, ground up and made into sticks with very little gum binder. There was no drying time and the images did not change over time like paint did, because no liquid was involved. Before she had tried oil paints, which took forever to dry, and required turpentine and linseed oil, much preparation, both before and after the painting itself. Then she worked with watercolors. She had to buy blocks of color and break them down one by one separately, adding water to get the right consistency. She'd spent a great deal of time working to get her colors similar each time, and storing them so they did not harden. She'd had to use linseed oil to seal and dry both oils and watercolors, and still they had faded. Pastels had been like a miracle. They let her work intuitively, freely, from the depth of her imagination, and she reveled in that freedom.

Chapter 5

Downstairs in the sitting room, Clare and Malcolm rocked in their chairs, the oil lamp low. He had just come in from a vicious night wind, and the howling was still in his ears.

"What did ye find out?" Clare asked as soon as he was warm and the wind shut away.

Malcolm removed his hat, revealing the chaos of his windblown hair. "He was at the baker's this mornin' first thing. Mistress Boyd said he lingered overlong, asked a question about our Caelia, but she pretended no' to hear. 'I'd no wish to be rude,' she said. 'Lord knows we welcome strangers here—though no' so willy-nilly as we did before the Forty-Five, m'lord. So I held my tongue, and ye ken tis no' an easy thing for me to do.' Introduced himself as Robert Hamilton."

Clare thought long and hard. "I've heard the name, but ne'er to fit a young man. Have ye?"

He shook his head. "No." He sat back in his chair. "Apparently only little Davy Fraser talked to him. I met him on the way home and he looked so troubled I stopped to see if I could help. He burst into tears and confessed he'd told the stranger all about his illness and Caelia's paintin'."

Her dark eyes softened and she half-smiled. "Poor bairn, grievin' like that for something so small. I'm glad he trusted ye. Mayhap he'll no' carry the guilt now."

Malcolm shared her bittersweet smile. "I think the shadow on his young soul has lifted."

They looked into each other's eyes for an instant, then glanced away without speaking. So much remained unsaid, unmentioned—for their protection and their slavish memories.

"They all trust ye," Clare murmured. "They know they can."

Malcolm tapped his empty pipe against his knee. As the local squire who lived at the manor house on the hill, he was both a gentleman and a kind and gentle man. He helped the tenants who farmed the oats, barley and rye that kept the glen running, along with sheep and some cattle and chickens. They had their own cows to provide the milk eggs and cheese they used. Clare herself had goats and chickens, but they got their beef and mutton from the tenants. Malcolm also bought from the families in the small town, usually without being asked. There was a mill, a seamstress, a blacksmith, and everyone wove their own cloth.

They rocked a while longer before Clare remarked, "I've thought and thought, and I just canna see. I wondered—" she broke off when her voice gave out, but she was not a weak woman. "I thought it might be..." she hesitated when she saw him tense for an instant. An instant only, and then it was gone, but she left the thought alone."

"He asked about her mam. And he told her things." He held his pipe and puffed, though he had not yet lit it. "It doesn't matter who he is. What're we goin' to do?"

"I can no' think."

He leaned forward, searching her dark brown eyes intently. "It may be time, Clare."

The sound of her name on his lips left a scar, as surely as if he'd sliced her with his fingernail. She didn't answer.

"You remember it all so clearly—still?" he asked as gently as he could.

"I've tried to forget, every hour, every day. But my life ended with the Forty-Five, and I can't." Her frustration, grief and sorrow dissolved the instant she saw the naked pain on his face.

For the second time in her life, Clare MacKinley was at a loss.

Malcolm took her hands and, for an instant, she let them rest in his open palms. But when his hands closed around hers, she withdrew, too quickly, like a sharp intake of breath.

~ * ~

Celia dreamed of a group of fairies hovering about her on iridescent wings. *But the fairies never come here anymore,* she tried to whisper, thrilled to be close to the tiny, fragile creatures. The vibration of wings made a song, and the song was rushed and noisy and piercing. She covered her ears, but the song grew louder. Suddenly they were gone and she was sorry she had spoken. Then, in an instant, the glen was still and welcoming, with the sound and the rhythm of the water in her ears. The valley spread out before her, glittering in the sun, the loch like a jewel at its heart. That's when it appeared: a shadow in the break between the loch and the forest. Somehow it was familiar.

She was awake in an instant, grabbing for the lamp, turning up the wick, falling to her hands and knees and searching for a particular sketchpad. She'd had that dream a week ago. She remembered it now in every detail. Quietly frantic, she pushed notebooks aside, flipped through a few pages, pushed aside more. Finally she found it far under the bed. She knew as soon as she touched it and a shock went up her arm.

Dragging it out, she hesitated, drew a deep breath, and turned to the last sketch in the pad. There it was, straight out of her dream. The glen was beautiful and still, the sun shown on the moor, and the lake was azure in the center of it all. But just at the point where the loch met the forest was a shadow—no. She was surprised to see she had drawn it quite clearly.

It was a man in a frockcoat, waistcoat, breeches and stockings. And his shadow fell so far and long that it touched every part of Glen Affric, splintering the stillness.

Chapter 6

The next morning Caelia was up early, as usual. By the time she was washed and dressed in a burgundy gown cut high across the bosom, and had braided her long hair, the sun was already shining through the lower portion of her bedroom window, having chased the mist away. It was always a good sign. She had dreamed about the fairies twice now. She couldn't help but smile, in spite of the shadow that had followed. She tried to force her feelings down, but failed miserably. She couldn't deny that the dream both exhilarated and frightened her.

She knelt to look through her window and saw the glen waiting, breath withheld, for someone to come enjoy it. This time she left her tools behind. She craved an early morning walk along the river.

By using the far staircase directly to the rear door past the kitchen, she took care not to wake Clare and Malcolm. She had heard them talking late last night and wanted them to rest. She threw her plaid around her shoulders as she stepped out onto the top of the hill: the highest in the glen, except for the mountains that ringed it. From where she stood the view of forest, moor, loch, river and distant purple mountains was gloriously alive. She took a deep breath of the misted mountain air. She felt a bit as if she were sneaking away from the lessons her aunt had given when she was younger, though she would never have thought of escaping then. She'd loved learning, and Clare had loved teaching. She'd wanted her niece to be well-read, to collect knowledge as she collected smooth round stones—to treasure and to make her more than she'd been born to be. She had always been an obedient child.

Tossing her thick braid over her shoulder, she started

across the moor to the private citadel where the sunlight blessed the water in patterns through the new spring leaves. She had not gone far when she noticed Robert Hamilton walking toward her.

Caelia paused, feeling ill—or not exactly ill, but jittery, or not exactly jittery, but distinctly odd. The one thing she did not feel was afraid. "Good morrow," she said formally when they stood near enough to speak.

"And to ye," he replied just as formally. He toyed with his tricorn hat for a moment, then burst out with, "I beg yer pardon for my behavior yesterday. Twas unconscionably rude, and ye'd been most polite and informative. I hope ye'll forgive me."

It was important to him; she could see that in the sincerity in his eyes and the way he clutched his hat in his fingers. "Perhaps," she said lightly, "if I understood why."

He sighed, released the pressure from his hat and shook his head. "I just…I was curious and I went too far."

Observing him, head tilted, she decided she could believe him. Almost. "Curious about what?" She wanted to sound skeptical, but only managed perplexed. Pulling her plaid closer, she waited.

Robert was becoming frustrated again, though he knew she had every right to question him. Or turn him away completely. But he couldn't let that happen. "About the odd name of yer house for one. Fairies' Haven? Tis a bit unrealistic, don't ye think?"

"Aye, but there's a legend about a fairy cave hidden beneath the big hill the house is built on." Somehow, to her astonishment, he had turned and they'd begun walking together. He offered her his arm, and, as if it were the most natural thing in the world (and not the first time it had happened to her), she took it, laying her palm on his fine wool frockcoat. She noticed his arm was firm and steady.

"Och, I see. A fairy cave, is it?" He found it difficult to sound the proper note of curiosity and skepticism, though he'd never believed in fairies and such like. "And where, exactly might this hidden cave be?" She smelled slightly of oranges, and the fragrance attracted him. Which was absurd. He'd known many beauties who would not turn him away. This girl-child, though 19-years-old, was a Highland country lass, naïve and, he suspected, ignorant of the ways of the world. Somehow that made him ache, and he did not like the feeling. And anyway, he had been the one to make a fool of himself at their last meeting, not she.

"Tis just the trouble. No one's been able to find it as far back as memory. The real name of the house is The Hill of the Hounds, from an incident in the 14th century, but the people *will* call it Fairies' Haven, no matter what we do. And anyway…" She trailed off, eyes full of sadness.

"What, Caelia Rose? Tell me." He really wanted to know, which surprised him. He frowned.

She took a deep breath and turned to catch him in her golden-brown eyes. "And anyway, the fairies have been gone for a long time."

Stopping short, he stared at her fixedly. "Surely ye're no' serious? Fairies don't exist."

She didn't flinch or look away or blush, but met his stare with gentle pity. "Tis what I thought ye'd say. But they do. And someday they'll come back. I know that, Robert Hamilton."

She removed her hand from his arm to find she missed its warmth.

"Even if they did, are ye no' afraid of them? They're supposed to be wily tricksters who only want to pull ye down into their world beneath the moss."

"Some of them, mayhap. But no' all," she replied too quickly, her desire to believe naked in her eyes.

He swallowed once, twice, caught in that golden-brown gaze. Covering her hand briefly with his, he shivered at the heat that raced across his palm. She must have felt it too, because her eyes widened in shock. She simply could not hide what she was feeling. He could not remember a time when he had been that young and carefree.

"Have ye looked for the cave?" he managed at last.

"Of course I looked. What fanciful child wouldn't? I searched and explored and climbed and fell, but never found a trace of the cave or the magic. The fairies took it with them."

He started to argue, but realized she was grinning just the slightest bit. He could not help but grin with her. "Perhaps I should help with the search. We might find it together."

She shook her head in regret. "We won't. Tis lost, ye see." She sounded disconsolate.

Robert shook himself internally. This was all well and good; getting her to talk to him, to talk about the secrets of this place. Perhaps now was the time to ask. "So even yer mother didn't know where the cave was?"

Caelia stopped, suddenly chilled, and stared at the mist-blurred colors of the springtime glen. The muted greens of the ferns and pines and birches and oaks, violets and fuchsias and whites of the flowers, the shimmering azure of the loch in the distance: they reminded her of a painting she had done years ago, in which the beauty of the glen was veiled behind a frail haze. She concentrated on the image, on the glen she loved, to ignore the irregular beat of her heart. "I told ye," she said with care, "no one has found it for a long, long time. Not even my mother."

"Ye say that as though, if anyone could have found it, she could."

Caelia took the risk of glancing at him out of the corner of her eye. His expression was merely curious; she could see no deception there. But she couldn't forget his questions the day before. "I believe that," she whispered. "She was charmed."

"Tell me about her," he said.

Her heart swelled with pride. She could not resist. "She was very beautiful—like a good fairy—and everyone loved her." It was a risk to continue, but she felt an unreasonable need to make this man understand how wonderful Lila Rose had been. "She was a hero in the Forty-Five, a spy for the Jacobites. She got vital information for them, and they might have won because of it, except for the Butcher."

She flushed and covered her mouth with her hands. She should not have revealed so much. She didn't even know this man. He was too young to have taken sides in the Jacobite rising but his family might have been on either side.

Caelia could not possibly remember those terrifying days, but her family had been Jacobites, and had told her stories of both the triumphs and disasters of the Forty-Five. She felt as though she had been there. If Robert Hamilton was like her, he had heard those tales as well. But from which perspective? Did he, like the others who sided with the British, believe the Highlanders were savages: brutal, uneducated, wild and uncontrollable?

Then it struck her; she did not care what he thought. She knew the truth, and that was all that mattered. She turned to meet his eyes; he was staring at her with a strange expression she could not read.

"Are ye sure?" His tone was emotionless.

Caelia was taken aback. "Of course I am." She paused. "About what?" This was not the response she had expected.

He ran his hand through his dark brown hair. "That she was…that yer mother was a spy for the Jacobites?" He meant to ask if she was a hero, but he couldn't quite say the word. Not when he had seen the glow on Caelia's face as she spoke of her mother, obviously much beloved.

She straightened her back and faced him squarely. "Aye. I could no' be more certain. Tis why the British killed her. They found out she'd betrayed them."

He hesitated, took a deep breath, and chose his answer

with great care. "Who told ye about what happened to Lila Rose?"

There was that toneless voice again. "My aunt. She was there. She saw it all." Why did she feel defensive suddenly? "And my father. He should know; he was married to her."

The silence that fell between them was filled with birdsong and the sighing wind, carrying the damp-scented air like a caress to their dew-wet faces.

Finally, pulse racing, palms damp, she began to speak, just to fill the uneasy stillness, already full of the glen and its songs.

Robert got there before her. "Did ye ever wonder if they might be mistaken?"

"Of course not. They're both very perceptive. They have my mother's letters. They're no' mistaken."

"Then mayhap they lied to ye." He said it very calmly, but he did not feel calm. Teeth gritted, he waited for her answer.

Heat rushed through her and she clenched her fists in rage. He was questioning everything she believed in. "They'd no' do that. They're good people, honest people. And ye, ye're just a stranger with no right to challenge me. Besides, ye were aye a bairn when Lila Rose died. Ye never knew her. They knew her from childhood—and loved her. Ye don't know Aunt Clare or Papa. Ye know nothin'!" She spat the words at him, trembling with anger.

"Or perhaps," he said so quietly she could barely hear him, "perhaps ye're just blind."

Caelia raised her head, her pulse racing, the words echoing in her mind. *Perhaps ye're just blind.* She had heard them before. Or something like them. More like, *Ye're blind!* But when? She couldn't remember. Or maybe she didn't want to. *Blind. Blind. Blind.* She wanted to cover her ears to shut out the sound, but it was already inside her. Besides, she didn't want him to see. "Ye'd best be goin' now."

The gold in her brown eyes had turned to ice that chilled him to the bone. He could no longer deny how deeply sad he felt at her distance and distress. His heart contracted painfully as he reached out to touch her arm. "I'm sorry, lass. Ye'll no' believe me, but I am."

Chapter 7

It took everything Caelia had to remain still until she was certain he was not coming back. Until he'd come—was it only yesterday?—she had never felt the need to prove anything to anyone, but now she was determined to show him she was not the fragile girl he thought her. And as for her parents....

Celia started to run back toward the Hill o' the Hounds. She wanted to dismiss everything Robert had said. She would forget it in the beauty of the glen she loved. She tried to call up the rain, spreading her arms as if she were capable of moving the heavens, but nothing happened. She was powerless after all. *And blind*, echoed again and again. *Perhaps ye're blind.*

"No," she cried to the cloudy sky. "I can see." She stopped to press the quaking leaf of a birch into her palm—new and soft and pale green—and then against her cheek. "I can feel, and smell." She sniffed the breeze that had whipped itself into a morning wind. Weeping like the *me'h'ing*—the mournful crying of the sheep. Raising her face to the rising wind, she let it sting her cheeks to remind her she was alive and whole, and that nothing had changed since she left the manor house that morning.

Except it had. *Are ye sure yer mother was a spy for the Jacobites?* Robert had asked. "Aye!" she shouted to the flurries of pale water on the loch, but the wind carried her voice away. She ran faster until the Hill loomed before her, safe and familiar. At least it used to be. *Perhaps they were mistaken?* His question followed her as she approached the grand entrance with the circled drive. *Or perhaps they were lying. They'd no' do that,* she'd replied. She believed it with all her heart.

Yet she went around the back of the long stone building and made her way up the outside stairs to the round tower on the southern end of the house. She had hidden the key behind a loose stone, which she removed, scraping her finger as she did so. *Ye see*, the voice inside said, *blind*. She ignored it and let herself in, locking the door behind her.

The tower door opened on the second floor hall with faded rose wallpaper and a worn Persian carpet. Since it was just the two Roses and Clare, they rarely used this part of the house, which had been built with thoughts of many children and at least three generations growing up within its walls. Silently she climbed to her room on the third floor, hoping desperately to avoid Clare and her father.

Caelia's cheeks flushed with guilt, but she couldn't face them now. Could it be she didn't trust them? Of course she did. Robert was the liar. Then why had he come here? And *why* had he lied? Instinctively, she went to her mother's trunk and retrieved from the carved chest the letters written back and forth between Lila and Clare.

They were sporadic, because Lila was never in the same place for long. At first she traveled with her father, trying to prepare men to rally to Prince Charles Stuart's banner when he landed in Scotland.

Once she carried a secret letter for her father to the Duke of Perth. He was so happy with her ingenuity, he asked her to carry a message to Prince Charles' lieutenant, Lochiel. She was thrilled. Caelia could tell from her mother's letters how Clare tried to talk her sister into stopping, how Lila seemed oblivious to the danger. Or else, she thrived on it; it seemed to feed some deep need in her that Clare couldn't understand—and feared deeply. The more Clare warned, the more Lila risked.

Caelia had delayed as long as she could. Finally she reached in and lifted out several drawings buried at the bottom of the chest. She sat with them on her lap for a moment, hesitant to turn the top one over.

Finally she did so, revealing the few attempts she had kept at creating her mother's likeness. She passed her hand over the unfinished pastel sketches. Time after time, she had drawn Lila Rose's lovely face—but the beauty stopped there. In one, what she had intended as flowering green vines had turned to snakes curling around Lila's head. In another, shadows obscured her delicate features to the point that she looked haunted, and her eyes were hollow. In a third, the moon, intended to shine benevolently on the background of the glen, instead had somehow wiped out the subtlety of greenery and life, leaving Lila's face in darkness. Caelia had tried again and again to capture her love and admiration for the woman who had been always ready to take wing, beautiful beyond words, completely irresistible and, in the end, a hero. So many efforts to put that delicately lovely face on paper: so many failures, so many papers, sketchpads, canvases destroyed.

She hid these drawings from her aunt and father, though she wasn't sure if it was from embarrassment or some other instinct. She felt she was somehow defiling her mother's memory. All she knew, intuitively, was they could not see these unfinished pieces.

Why did the ugliness always come? It worried her—this inability to capture in pastel the woman she loved and admired so much. Everything else she painted was true. She'd learned that over the years in various ways. She didn't know why it happened, why the truth poured out of her pastels; she just knew it did. But not this time. Unless... *Perhaps ye're blind.*

"Unless he's right." She mouthed the words but gave them no sound. No, that was not the answer. Who was he, after all, to know the first thing about her mother? To accuse her parents of lying? And why did he care? All she knew was, now that he had asked the questions, she had to know answers.

Her fingers itched to sketch, as did her instincts, but she forced those feelings down. The last thing she wanted to see right now was the truth in pastel colors.

Afraid of the truth, are ye?

He had not said it out loud, but his eyes as much as challenged her with the unspoken words.

"Yes," she admitted in the slightest whisper. "I'm afraid."

Her eyes filled with tears that did not fall, because she dared not let them. Lips pressed together to keep her confusion, doubt and fear from flying out, she put the sketches back in their hiding place. Then she did what she had wanted to do since Robert Hamilton had started asking his venomous questions two hours since. She went to her bed, kicked off her brogues, and curled up in a tight, trembling ball.

Chapter 8

Something woke Caelia from her trance-like state. Slowly she uncurled her body like a new formed butterfly breaking free of its chrysalis. Feeling as awkward as she imagined that small creature would feel, she stretched out, the folds of her crumpled gown spreading like the fresh, wrinkled wings of a damp butterfly. Every movement hurt as if her muscles were unsullied and unused, like her thoughts and questions and newborn doubts.

She did not open her eyes, because she did not want to see. Not yet. Perhaps not ever. *Dear God, what has this stranger done to me?* she wondered.

Moving her arms to the rhythm of her pulse, she beat at the air to swat her aching doubts away. But they did not go. Soon she crossed her arms on her chest and lay quiet and still.

Malcolm Rose climbed the stairs to Caelia's room and stopped in the doorway, frightened for an instant by the pale and motionless pose in which she lay. She must not have heard Clare call her for dinner. His daughter's beauty and innocence, the straight line of her mouth and her vulnerability caught him. *I'm so proud of ye*, mo-run, he thought. *I'd do anything to protect ye.* His eyes burned.

Clare thought she heard her father speaking, or perhaps it was only a dream. At last she opened her eyes. She sat up abruptly and spread her arms wide. "Papa!"

In a blur he sat on the edge of her bed and hugged her tight, while she hugged him tighter. The fatherly embrace lasted a long time—so long, and she held on so tight, that he became concerned.

Caelia was reluctant to let him go. Reluctant to pull

away from him and look him in the face. Reluctant to search his beloved features for the cracks and chinks she suspected existed. *Ye're wrong*, she told herself silently. *Robert is wrong. This is the man I've know all my life. The man who has encouraged me and loved me and kept me safe.* But still she didn't let him go.

Finally, he broke away, stroking her hair with affection. "Cook has supper waitin', and she'll be in a temper if we're no' there as soon as soon as may be."

"Clare's there as well, aye?"

"Aye," he said, "isna she always?" Something in her tone made him uneasy.

"Aye, always." Caelia smiled, her eyes unreadable, rose and took her father's arm. "Then tis down we go."

They walked thus, arm-in-arm down the burgundy-carpeted stairway to the mahogany table set for three where Clare was waiting.

When they finished their mutton chops with potatoes and cabbage, as well as oatcakes with sweet spices and cream, Cook disappeared into the kitchen, where she would be clanging pots and pans and china for far longer than was strictly necessary. Caelia put aside her linen napkin—only slightly frayed at the edges—and carried the tea things into the sitting room, where a low fire burned.

Clare and Malcolm relaxed in their wing-backed chairs, allowing their usually straight spines to slacken and their shoulders to fall with the release of their deep breaths. Both smiled at Caelia as she poured tea into three pottery mugs and added a bit of milk and a bit of sugar. They liked to watch the graceful way she moved about, her light-brown hair swaying as she moved. Their worries always lightened when the three were together like this in the cozy sitting room of the over-large manor house.

Passing out the mugs, the girl found her favorite spot on the rug near the hearth and cleared her throat. "I saw

Robert Hamilton this mornin'," she announced baldly. "We talked about the fairy cave."

Clare, who was very good at hiding her thoughts, forgot to do so. Her alarm was evident in her thinned lips and slightly widened eyes.

Malcolm was more relieved than anything. Until his daughter continued.

"He asked about my mother, about Lila again." She folded her hands together, fingers pressing into the backs. "He wanted to know if I was sure she was a spy for the Jacobites. He asked if perhaps ye were mistaken about it." She barely got out the last three words, her throat was so dry.

A long silence followed, broken only by the cheerful crackling of the fire.

"Why would he ask— Ye talked to him about the Forty-Five? Ye know that's dangerous, even now." Malcolm heard what he was saying, but he barely understood it. His forehead was beaded with perspiration and his palms damp.

The color drained from Clare's face and she stared at her niece blankly.

"I know twas foolish, but I'd no' the power to stop. Tis no' the point in any case. Could ye have been mistaken? Ma-clare?"

Clare winced at the endearment. "Mistaken?" she echoed. "No." She wanted to gather Caelia in her arms and hold her tight enough to squeeze these perilous questions out of her. She wanted to sing soft lullabies in her ear as she had when Caelia was a small child, to soothe away the suspicion and dread. She wanted to tell the girl she loved her as deeply as, if not deeper than her own child, that Robert Hamilton was mistaken. She wanted to, so much that her heart ached to bursting, but she couldn't.

Caelia was only more perplexed by her aunt's pale skin and odd expression, and by her father's glassy stare.

"Caelia, *mo-cridhe*, ye have to understand twas desperate and confusin' back then. Hard to know what anyone truly believed. Twas—"

"I'll tell ye this," Clare choked out, "whatever yer mother believed, it had nothin' to do with Robert Hamilton. He could no' have been more than a bairn in '46. What makes him ask ye these things? What makes ye think he knows the answers?"

"Because," Caelia responded shakily, "when I asked just now, ye both looked ill." She took a deep breath that made her ache from her chest to the bottom of her belly. "Tis time to tell me the truth."

Chapter 9

Pacing in front of the tiny fire in his uncomfortable room in the town of Beauly, Robert Hamilton rubbed his dry, burning eyes. He knew there was a dispatch for him, but he had not picked it up. He had no wish to read it at the moment.

In just his shirt and breeches, he traipsed back and forth, restless and troubled. He could not believe how little Caelia knew about her own birthright, how naïve she was, and willing to reveal her ignorance and naiveté. He did not like to admit how deeply both touched him. He was used to worldly women, who knew far too much about far too many trite and dangerous things. They themselves were dangerous in that knowledge.

But Caelia Rose was dangerous to no one but herself.

And him.

She was so honest that he winced at the thought of her decency. It made him throb with desire and remorse. He no longer remembered what it felt like to be himself. He had become so accustomed to duplicity it was now second nature to him. He yearned for her clear and trusting vision: something he would never know again. He yearned for her warm, sweet lips. He yearned for her to take him back to the days when he believed in love and honor and loyalty.

Raising his head suddenly, he stared at the dying flames in accusation. "I'd no' be knowin' if I can do it."

But she deserves the truth, the fire seemed to reply.

"Does she?" he whispered. "Or is't just that I can't have her without it?"

~ * ~

The fire flickered and danced, casting cheerful shadows over Caelia where she sat on the floor. She waited, aware of every hiss and spark of the flames, of every heavy breath her father and aunt took. They were breathing in tandem, as if they shared but one set of lungs. They glanced at each other once, asking silent questions in unspoken desperation, but neither moved. They were frozen in time, disbelieving at what had come to pass.

They should have been prepared for this, the girl thought, *should have known this moment would come someday. How odd that they should be so close in this critical moment, so exactly alike*. The firelight did not reach their faces—nor the shadows—and the mist shrouded the sun outside the row of French windows. The blue and red Persian rug and dark upholstery on the chairs and settee only emphasized the dimness, and the blank look in their eyes.

Finally Malcolm knelt beside her, wincing at the pain in his arthritic knees. He took her hands, which lay unresponsive in his. "Caelia, tis no so bad as ye think. Twas so dark, yet hopeful a time back then. One day there was joy because Prince Charles had taken Carlisle, Manchester and Preston in England, the next despair, because he had turned back toward Scotland. The Sassenach army had been here since the '15, buildin' their roads and their cannon and tryin' to impose their heartless kind of order. We all hated them—most all anyway. No' the Campbells, of course. They fought on the side of George II, and after Culloden, helped the Butcher with his massacre. The British were always stronger than us. And ye know the Grants and the Gordons split to fight on both sides."

"But we had the passion, *mo-run*, and the love of our land and heritage above all things." Clare joined them on the floor, her skirts rustling as she settled onto the carpet. "Ye understand that passion, because ye share it, Caelia."

"Aye, tis true. But what's that to do—"

"The Roses refused to fight at all. Hugh Rose of Kilravok declared the clan neutral."

"Ye never told me that!"

"It didn't really matter. I could no' stay at home tendin' cattle and crops. So I joined Charles Edward Stuart in his cause. But I was wounded at Stirling and had to come home. I hated to go, but I needed to survive. For Lila and Clare."

Shaking her head, Caelia tried to understand.

Clare put her hand on her niece's knee. "He just wants ye to know how bewilderin' it all was, how wrenchin' for the men who must follow their laird into a battle they no' believed in. How allegiances shifted, were cemented, shifted again as Prince Charles changed tactics and the British army grew stronger. Ye ken while she was collectin' intelligence for us, yer mother was kidnapped by a British major-general and held captive. How he forced her to become his lover."

Caelia tensed, feeling ill. "He raped her." She glanced at her father, but it was Clare who nodded sharply. "'Twas well into the Risin' by then, and she was carryin' ye, as ye know. We think…Malcolm and I think she gave in to her despair. 'Twas too horrible for her. She gave up."

"'Twas why we think she worked for both sides, lass. He made her tell him everything she knew, that cruel major-general." Malcolm blinked dry eyes that were suddenly damp. "But that doesn't diminish what she did for the Jacobites."

"Of course it does. It means she was no' the woman I thought she was. It means she was a coward and a traitor.

"The English would have called her a traitor anyway." Clare seemed to have trouble speaking the words.

"Ye're playin' games with words. Neither side could trust her." Tears filled Caelia's throat and she almost choked on them. "And *ye* could no' trust *me* enough to tell me the truth."

"The truth is never simple," her father murmured. "We didn't want to complicate things. Ye see, no one is perfect. We're all flawed. We wanted ye to love her and think well of her."

"Mayhap in the beginnin', when I was too young to understand. But why not tell me as I grew? I feel like a fool, like ye thought twould break me, like ye think of me still as a child."

All at once she straightened her back and made them look into her eyes. "If Mr. Hamilton hadn't come along, would ye ever have told me the truth?"

They started to answer at the same time, then both stopped. She could tell they didn't want to lie to her again.

She could not face them any longer—not while her heart was breaking. She rose carefully, avoiding their gazes and their reaching hands, crossed the carpet and went up to her room.

Once alone, she thought she would feel relieved, but she didn't. She felt lost and bereft. Instinctively, she opened Lila's chest and lifted out the abandoned sketches.

Caelia knew, or thought she did, that everyone had human frailties. Was spying for the enemy—the cruel and unjust, vicious enemy—evil enough to explain the ugliness that came into her pastels each time she tried to sketch mother?

Caelia had always been sad that she wasn't more like her mother, but just now she was glad. She flushed with guilt at the thought. She would never betray Scotland or those she loved. She knew it in her soul, deeply and without question. She had seen the pain in her father's eyes, in Clare's, when they admitted what Lila had done. It had broken their hearts as well. Perhaps, after all, they had meant well by keeping their secret. Perhaps.

Dropping the drawings, Celia picked up a sketchbook and a mirror (not the one framed by silver lace) settled on the windowseat and did a quick drawing of her face.

Instinctively, she began to sing one of the songs from The Tea Cup Miscellany to the tune of "Auld Lang Syne".

When flow'ry meadows deck the year,
And sporting lambkins play,
When spangl'd fields renewed appear,
And music wak'd the day;
Then did my Chloe leave her bow'r,
To hear my am'rous lay:
Warm'd by my love, she vow'd no Pow'r
Shou'd lead her heart astray.

Usually these efforts became interesting impressions with a touch of the mystical, like the one she had painted the previous morning, before she met the stranger who had changed her life with but a few questions. She bent her head to the drawing and sang in her sweet soprano voice.

Joy transporting never fails
To fly away as air,
Another swain with her prevails
To be as false as fair.
What can my fatal passion cure?
I'll never woo again;
All her disdain I must endure,
Adoring her in vain.

When the song ended and her pastels grew still, she saw the drawing was vague, without shape or real contour, and it looked like no one at all.

So today her mother was less of an illusion and more of an actual person, while somehow Caelia was less.

She put down her pastels and paper and wept.

Chapter 10

She dreamed of the fairies again, only this time she couldn't remember the dream when she awoke. She only knew, as she grabbed some fresh bannocks and crowdie from the kitchen, that those fragile fairy wings seemed to be pushing her out the door. Pushing her toward discovery.

She felt betrayed by her parents—for she thought of Clare as a parent as much as she did her father. They had no faith in her, it seemed, yet handsome Robert Hamilton had asked her directly, right away, as if he believed she would know, or should.

The vast sky arcing over moor and river was moody, with heavy thunderclouds that left shadows racing over the long, pale grass. Patches of blue broke through here and there, making promises of sun and spring that Caelia only half believed. She wore a peach gown with a simple over-robe embroidered in rust flowers, and had twined her hair into one thick braid tied with a peach ribbon. She felt pretty; she needed to feel pretty to overshadow her doubts and misgivings.

Though the design on her rust leather slippers was as decorative as her gown, they were sturdy and would take her safely most anywhere in Glen Affric. Today she was headed for the river.

Robert found her there, picking her way among the layers of circular flat rocks, stained rust to orange to gold to sparkling silver. The peat-colored river, which had shaped and colored them, rushed past, leaving ferns and reeds and lichen drenched in its path. He noticed Caelia was listening, as if to a symphony. "Ye look lovely today, Mistress Rose," he said, bowing. "I hope I've no' disturbed yer sleep with my pointed questions yesterday."

She paused, but only briefly. "I'll never feel the same again, about anything, and that hurts, Mr. Hamilton."

"Aye, growin' up often does."

"Tis what I feared." Her lips trembled through her smile, but she straightened her shoulders and threw her head back. "But I ne'er want to feel the fool again."

Without warning, he took her hand and kissed it with his warm lips, sending chills along her arms. "Ye're a brave girl, Caelia. And I'm sorry tis me who's causin' ye pain."

She did not know how to reply. The light touch of his fingers caused sensations to course through her body that bewildered her. The memory of his determination the day before perplexed her. She could not think straight at all with him hovering so near, confusing her senses. "Tis no' ye. Tis the lies." She fell silent, then, "Why have ye come?" she asked.

"I thought today I'd help ye search for the fairy cave."

She blinked twice at the frustration that shattered her hard-won calm. "No, I meant—"

"I know what ye meant, but I'll no' be talkin' of that today. Today is for discoveries, dear Caelia, and for pleasure. Tis the least I can do to make up for havin' upset ye. No drama today, do ye agree?"

She withdrew her hand from his and smoothed her gown while she considered. She had set out this morning intending to be troubled, but the fairies had not liked that, she knew. That's why they'd been pushing her, were pushing even now, for her to go exploring. She shook her head forcefully. *The fairies are gone. Why do I keep forgettin'?* What was it Robert had said? *Today is for discoveries.* Could he have known what she was thinking? No, she decided, it was pure coincidence. She decided Robert was right. It was time for some amusement. "If ye're goin' to continue to be rude and insist upon orderin' me about, then I suppose I have no choice." But she gave him a half-smile as she said it.

They headed toward the base of the hill on which the Hill o' the Hounds sat. It seemed higher to Caelia today, and harder to reach. A catch in her throat made her pause and blink away threatening tears. She would not show Robert her weakness again.

She followed him, amused that he felt he could lead such an expedition. His clothes were far too fine for climbing about among the birch copses and broad aged oaks. The pale green ferns and celandine clung to his breeches and stockings, leaving ghostly marks in moisture on his legs. His longish brown hair, originally held back with a stamped leather tie, was soon hanging about his face and straggling over the collar of his frockcoat, while Caelia ducked in and out with ease.

She knew this place quite as well as she loved it.

When Robert looked back, he could have sworn the branches of the oaks rose to let her pass effortlessly, and the shivering leaves of the birches and thick ferns took in a breath, so they scarcely brushed her lovely skirt. He shook his head, catching it on another twig, while his foot became tangled in a stalk of purple foxglove. *Who's having delusions now?* he asked himself.

He hurried on, pushing aside young, narrow birches to get as close to the hill as he could. Brow furrowed, he scanned the hillside ahead and behind, looking for an anomaly that might reveal one fold too many, or the hint of an indentation. Once he caught Caelia smiling at him and could not resist smiling back.

They stayed where they were, motionless, for a long moment, grinning like miscreant children. Suddenly he took her hand and helped her over a slanted, protruding boulder. She did not withdraw her hand at once, but stared at the boulder, then up at the hanging ivy interspersed with honeysuckle.

"I never noticed this before. Do ye think that rock is a marker of some kind?" she asked.

"Aye." His eyes were still on her, but he forced himself to look where she was pointing. The boulder was too flat and rounded to be accidental. "Shhh!" he whispered as he began to move forward slowly along the narrow path at the base of the tall hill. With Caelia close beside him, he slid his hands through strands of ivy and fragrant honeysuckle, feeling the rock face beneath.

"We need no' be still," Caelia said. "I told ye they've gone." She moved her hands behind Robert's, loving the feel of the long, swaying strands and the tiny white flowers that smelled so sweet. She did not remember seeing this place before: the flat curved boulder and the ivy and flowers falling like nature's tresses over the hillside. She did not remember the way the rock turned inward just there, where the ferns grew so tall they reached her shoulders. All her life she had lived at Fairies' Haven, and never had she felt this close to discovering the magic cave. Her pulse raced with anticipation.

"I'm thinkin' tis what we seek, Caelia Rose. Take care where ye put yer feet."

All at once they were inside the curtain of greenery, where dim colored light filtered through. A tall boulder—taller by three feet than Robert—blocked their way, but he was undaunted. He pushed his whole body against it and it moved slightly. "Caelia—"

She didn't wait for him to finish. "I'll try the other." They pushed from various angles, with very little movement, and then, suddenly, the giant stone swung smoothly, admitting them into a cool, dark cave.

The longer Caelia stood, holding her breath, the more color she recognized in the dimness. There was light coming from somewhere, though she couldn't tell from which direction. She was barely aware of Robert stopping beside her, so enraptured was she by the view.

Curved walls covered with pale and darker green moss circled what looked like the outside walls of the cave, while inside were circling pillars of pale green and lilac. Somehow, the light changed, and even the green was touched with purple toward the top. Green and lightening shades of lilac intertwined toward the base. A small stream split off into three through a low waterfall, tinged purple mixed with gold, and the earthen rust of the peat-colored water. Somehow, the walls and water shimmered, dreamlike, and splintered patterns of light danced from ceiling to gold-flecked floor and back again. This place made her rejoice.

"How is't ye knew how to find the cave?" She was consumed with curiosity.

"I didna. Ye saw how many times we circled before the openin' appeared. It took perseverance, twas all."

Called by the sound of the rippling spring, she turned, hearing within it a voice that had told her long ago, "Only the blessed can find the fairy cave; tis no' for the likes of ordinary mortals." *But Robert's ordinary. He doesn't even believe in magic. So why was he able to lead me here?* "We're normal, ye and me, are we no'?" She believed that—and wished for it—with all her heart. Though she'd always wanted to follow in the blithe footsteps of her mother, she knew that was never to be. Caelia loved her home, her safety, her certainty too much. She loved every tree and flower and blade of grass in the glen Lila Rose had so casually left behind. More than that, Caelia loved the water: still or rushing, silent or singing, and the clear remarkable light.

"No, lass." Robert took her hand to lead her over some slick, worn stones. The feeling of her hand in his sent tingles up his arm. "Ye're anything but ordinary. In fact ye're quite exceptional."

She stopped and faced him, but did not take her hand away. "Ye needn't say so as balm to my feelin's. I know what I am."

It was his turn to stare. "Caelia, dear lassie, I don't

think ye do. And I wish so much ye did."

Waving his reassurance aside as if it were a wasted kindness, she drew him deeper among the multi-hued pillars. She still did not retrieve her hand.

Caelia was intrigued when she saw a decaying wooden platform against an outside wall. Here and there, fragments of a rotted woolen blanket clung to it. Feeling a jolt of recognition, she turned to Robert, eyes wide.

"I've been here before," she murmured, afraid to shatter the glimmering stillness of the enchanted cave.

"But ye told me ye never had."

"Aye, I'd forgotten. Twas long, long ago, when I was very wee, I'm thinkin'." She had forgotten because Clare and her father had made her forget, and she hadn't wanted to remember.

~ * ~

"Mistress MacKinley, Master Rose, they're comin'!" someone had screamed on that long ago day. "Ye'd best get ye away and hide."

Caelia had been so little she didn't remember their faces, but she remembered the terror in their voices.

"Who's coming?" someone cried, as the little girl clung to her aunt's skirts.

"The Butcher's men! The English! We must hide. They'll burn the house and the crops, ye ken. They always do."

"Make sure the guns are well hidden!" Malcolm Rose called out, his tone relatively calm, though threaded through with dread.

Caelia clung tighter as people swirled around her like the loch in a storm. She was terrified she'd get swept away and drowned.

"But where?" her aunt Clare whispered.

Caelia had never heard her voice shake like that before.

"We've no choice but to find the fairie cave," Cook shouted, white apron billowing.

Clare shook her head. "It doesn't exist. Tis just a folktale."

"Tisn't," proclaimed a new voice: male, though not as mature as the men rushing about. "Follow me. I can show ye. We've just time if we hurry!"

Caelia was mesmerized by the boy's bright red hair. She'd never seen the like before. She didn't know where the boy had come from, but heard several people call him Red Rory. They said his name with a reverence that confused her. He was a bairn like she was, though bigger, and he certainly shone brighter. Everyone followed him as if he were laird.

She thought she could hear hoofbeats all around as Clare picked her up and they bounced along the hillside behind Red Rory's flaming hair. The girl could smell the dust the English horses were churning up; it was choking her. She could hear their harsh, threatening voices and feel the points of their bayonets. There was gunpowder in the air; she was sure of it, though the British were not yet in sight. She thought her little heart would burst with the panic her parents had planted there.

So suddenly that it left her dazed, she was surrounded by cool, enveloping darkness, by soft voices whispering with relief. Suddenly there were reflections on the ceiling—purple light and soft green walls and lilac fading down into the golden stones beneath. Everyone crouched against a long, curved wall. Clare and Malcolm, Caelia on their lap, sat on a blanket-covered platform to keep them from the chill.

Caelia looked about for Red Rory, but he was gone, and everyone else was waiting. She felt the suspense like heavy hands upon her shoulders, though she was entranced by the sparkling water reflected in shifting fragments of light upon the ceiling. It was almost enough to distract her altogether. For a long time no one moved or spoke; they scarcely even breathed.

Caelia was unable to hear or see or guess what was happening outside. All she knew was that they were in a sacred place and she prayed the magic would follow them when they went outside.

Finally she heard a sharp, high whistle, and everyone rose soberly, waiting for a sign of Red Rory. A flash of his hair and he waved them out, though the child realized he kept his face hidden under his soft leather cap.

"Malcolm." Clare put her hand on her brother-in-law's arm to stop him when he took his first step. "I can't...I don't want to see what they've left in their wake."

Malcolm put his arm around her and squeezed, but his eyes were full of sadness.

When they stepped beyond the curve of the hill, they gasped. Caelia stood between them, swinging her head this way and that. The house was still standing, as were the fields of oats and barley, and the cattle pens and the sheep on the hill. Smoke curled up from two haystacks their enemies had burned, and one old cow lay slaughtered beside them.

In great trepidation, they all went back to the manor house to find it undisturbed, except for one bottle of wine that had been drunk and a couple of bannocks eaten.

Clare went pale. "Are ye sure twas the Butcher's men? They destroy everything they touch."

Red Rory was gone, but one of the farmers had seen them coming close up. "Aye, so twas."

"Red Rory, was it? He got about, did Rory, tryin' to help when he could."

Chapter 11

The thought, and the sound of Robert's voice, brought her sharply back to the present.

Caelia blinked to clear her vision and her memory. Robert's attractive face—his wide cheekbones, chiseled chin and straight nose, surrounded by strands of dark brown hair—came into immediate focus. But her memories did not fade. "He saved a good many lives and a good bit of silver from the rampages of the British army." She paused to smooth the skirt of her gown. "Ye know about Red Rory?" That was important.

"Who in the Highlands doesn't?"

She stared at him curiously. "Aye, but twas a long time ago."

When she stepped on an uneven boulder and wobbled, he took her elbow gently. "He's a legend, ye ken, who came right after the Forty-five. He's no' easily forgotten."

"He was aye young to be such a hero. I was so little. Do ye ken his age at the time?" She thought Robert must have been around the Highlands 16 years ago, or he wouldn't know about this boy.

"They say he was nine or ten."

Her aunt and her father had never spoken again about that day or Red Rory, so Caelia had only hearsay to go on. But the boy had been a favorite Highland hero during the desperate days when The Duke of Cumberland, King George II's brother, had slashed and burned his way through the Highlands and Islands after the tragic battle at Culloden Moor. He and his men had hunted down fleeing soldiers and burned them in the houses where they hid. They had put too many great houses to the torch, and murdered too many Jacobites in an effort to restore order to

58

a place already destitute and defenseless.

Child that he was, Rory had taken it upon himself to warn those he could, to whisk them out of harm's way, so even if Cumberland destroyed their crops and took their jewels, at least he did not get their lives. The boy was a beam of light and hope in the midst of smothering darkness.

"What happened to him in the end? Did the English ever catch him?" she asked.

Robert could tell she really wanted to know, that she cared about the stranger who had saved so many. Her eyes were meltingly brown with just a hint of gold and he felt himself falling into their depths. But he could not help feeling there was something else on her mind, something she had not spoken of when she told the story of her family's escape from the British forces. "No one knows what happened to him, but they love to speculate."

Caelia thought of the fear that day. The way Papa and Ma-clare refused to speak of it ever again. Her dry eyes stung when she looked up. "There's more they've no' told me, isn't there?"

He could not bear the sadness in her face. Unwittingly, she had put her hand on his chest in an appeal he could not resist. "Aye, so there is."

He was certain she was going to cry, but she blinked away her tears, just as she'd tried to blink away her memories a few minutes past. "Caelia, I wish—"

"What, Robert? What is't ye wish?"

She swayed closer, until he could feel her warm breath in a rush against his face.

"I can't promise ye..." His pulse raced at her nearness, at her vulnerability and her willingness to stand so close. Her lips were slightly parted.

"Then don't. Just..." She raised her chin, shocked by her behavior. He aunt had taught her well; her father had warned her of men who could not be trusted. Of their vague needs and yearnings, of the danger in giving them their way.

The two stared at each other for a long moment, then Robert touched her cheek with his fingertips. "Caelia."

She nodded and stood on tiptoe, pressing her breasts against his chest as he slid his arm around her. Heat rushed through her body, surprising, then engaging her. "Kiss me," she whispered.

He drew her close and lowered his lips to her soft pink ones. They were warm, and they met his eagerly. He was rocked by the sensations she let loose in him. Was it her tender innocence? Her soft beauty? Or her willing, inexperienced embrace? He did not care. Her nearness was intoxicating, like fine light wine that crept into a man's brain slowly, ever so slowly, until he could no longer stand. He burned for her, and yet he wanted only this tender kiss, this soundless meeting of her full young body against his. He was aroused and desperate, but would not, for all his world-weary experience and knowledge of things dark and painful, hurt her in this moment by asking for more than she could give.

The kiss alone was a gift beyond price, and when he drew away, he saw she was grateful and disappointed at the same time.

With both hands on his waistcoat, Caelia shivered, though she knew she was safe, even here, alone with this stranger in this sacred place of light and water and color and motion,.

"We should go," he said.

She nodded, unable to find the words.

As they stepped outside, treading carefully along the rocky ledge, the mist rose around them. The sun had disappeared behind dark clouds just visible beyond the thick veil. It began to rain. Caelia reached for her plaid to draw it over her head, realizing only then that she had left it at home. How odd. She never forgot her plaid.

Before she could lower her arms, Robert took off his frock coat, insisting she wear it. "A plaid's no real protection against a Highland shower anyway."

She tried to resist, but the scent of him seduced her into sliding her arms into the wide, long sleeves.

They continued to walk as if it weren't raining. Both knew it would stop soon. Robert was anxious to make conversation. "I did hear once, about Red Rory, that in a close call with a British officer, he was cut with a heated sabre on his shoulder."

"I heard it too, but twas his ear, and the mark turned the hair it touched to a streak of white, tellin' everyone who came near he was a hero."

Robert looked skeptical. "Sounds overly romantic to me." His mind was racing. What on earth would he do now?

Caelia stopped in front of him and blocked his path. "Ye don't believe in romance, then, laddie?" She smiled and her face lightened with glee.

He wanted to kiss her again, but they were out in the open, and the depth and beauty of her teasing smile frightened him. More, even, than his guilt. *I must be mad to think of brushin' her cheek with my fingers, of curlin' them in her soft shinin' hair. But to remember that kiss... No! I can no' let this happen.* Yet it had. He could neither deny it nor his desire to make it happen again.

They walked on in silence. It was not far to the path worn deep into the stone of the hill.

By accident she slipped her hand into his coat pocket as she struggled to get the over-large garment off.

He reached out blindly, but she was already pulling a brass button into her palm.

"What's this?" she asked, because she did not know what else to say. She noticed the kid covered buttons on his frock coat. His waistcoat fasteners were made of ivory.

He replied without thinking. "I found it lyin' in the

road and picked it up from habit."

"Ye make a habit of pickin' things up from the road?" She squinted up at him, then back at the brass button. "Besides, it's not very dusty."

He held his voice even. "I shined it up before I put it in my pocket."

"Oh, aye." She wondered how she was speaking clearly—or at all. She too was thinking only of the kiss. She dropped the button back into the pocket as she finally got free of his coat. By the time she returned it to him, she had steadied her hands and her expression. "Thank ye for this. And...everything." She stood silent for a long time, but there was nothing else to say. Finally she turned and climbed toward her home.

This time *he* stayed to watch *her* go, aching from every memory the day had brought. And wondering nervously how long it would be before she guessed what she should never know.

Chapter 12

Caelia slipped into the house through the tower once more and went straight to her room, where she began to rifle through her old sketchbooks. She'd remembered as she climbed the outer stairs that years after the soldiers and Red Rory came, she'd done some sketches of several memories of the day. She'd felt driven to sketch them, though she wasn't certain why. She only knew she had to find them now.

When she realized she was turning her neat piles into chaos, she stopped to think. It had been two years ago when she felt the urge to put those memories on paper. She went to a stack in the corner, drenched in dust, just below the painted burn coming down the wall. Using her petticoat, she cleaned off the dust, which exploded in mist-muted air. Then she flipped through the top three, coming at last to a series from that fearful day: Red Rory, his hair gleaming in the sun, his hand raised to urge the people forward; inside the fairy cave, with the shaded color and dancing light, somewhat dimmed by a breath of fear; the table with the empty wine bottle and bannock crumbs on a handkerchief, and a woman's hand reaching in....

When she touched the image it expanded in a flash. Clare reached in, diving suddenly for the handkerchief, crumpling it until it was too small to see, and stuffing it into her bodice.

Now Caelia understood why she had made this sketch.

Malcolm was out working with the tenants, but Clare was waiting for her niece when she sat down at the table. For supper they had beef brose and trout with browned tatties, but Caelia ate very little.

Clare watched her niece throughout the meal, noticing her pale cheeks and disinterest as she toyed with her food. Clare could see the depth of the emotions crossing Caelia's face, but she could not read them, and that was unusual. The girl she knew was open and had no secrets, or so her aunt had always believed. But Caelia had changed since Robert Hamilton appeared in Glen Affric. *Malcolm must make him go*, she thought, not for the first time. She also noticed her niece was watching her furtively, a question in her eyes. "What ails ye, *mo-run*," she asked when she could no longer bear the suspense.

Startled, Caelia dropped her fork, along with all pretense that she was hungry, or even knew what food was on her plate. Though it was difficult, she gazed at her aunt eye to eye. "Ye've heard of Red Rory?"

It was Clare's turn to clatter her fork against her plate, though she kept a grip on it. She cleared her throat and tried to still her churning insides. "Aye, I've heard the name."

"They say he was famous when I was younger." Caelia could not miss her aunt's discomfort with the subject. "For rescuin' Jacobites from the British."

"Oh, aye, I've heard of his exploits." Clare's voice was calm now, though her expression was still tense. "He warned Jacobite soldiers when the Duke of Cumberland was coming, and kept them from being burned alive. And later, when the wearin' of the plaid and the speakin' of the Gaelic and the playin' of the pipes was proscribed by the British, the Highlanders had small n's where they revived our culture, dancin' and singin' and exultin' in the old ways. Sometimes Red Rory would hear that the army had caught wind of the celebrations, and he'd warn the Highlanders. By the time the British arrived, there'd be naught but some fire rings smolderin'."

Caelia smiled, misty-eyed. "I'd love to go to one of those celebrations, wouldn't ye?"

For once Clare let down her guard: the carefully

constructed wall that protected her from wanting things she could not have and mourning things she had lost. Only her niece had the power to make her do that. "Aye, twould be lovely to spend a day or two in the past and pretend twas the present."

The contentment in her voice brought tears to Caelia's eyes. "Twould indeed, Ma-clare." She took a few bites of her fish to give herself courage; it was so difficult to confront her aunt when she was lost in a brief moment of pleasure. Yet ask she must; she must know. "I was thinkin' of Red Rory that day the English came when I was aye a bairn. Twas he who hid us."

Clare stiffened, feeling ill, and remained silent.

"Why did they no' burn the house and crops?"

"I'd not know what the soldiers were thinkin'. The Butcher was long back in England. Mayhap they'd grown weary of burnin' by then."

Caelia did not believe her. "I think ye do know." She spoke softly, but the challenge was there. "I saw ye hide the handkerchief ye found on the table."

"How could ye? Ye were so wee!" Clare exclaimed, and then covered her mouth with her hand.

Squeezing her aunt's other hand, Caelia tried to suppress her curiosity and sense of dread. "I saw it in a paintin'. Please tell me."

Clare shivered, but whether at the thought of the "seeing" or the truth about the handkerchief, she did not know. *I wish Malcolm were here. But he isn't*. This was one choice she would have to make on her own. She pushed her half-finished trout away and took a deep breath. "Caelia, lass, tis true I took the handkerchief. I burned it. I knew what it meant, why the house and everything else had been spared before I saw the initials." She spoke slowly and with care. "It told me the raid had been led by Major-General Jonathan Kingston. No doubt he was told to do it, but couldn't because…" She stumbled, took another breath.

"Have I no' heard that name before?" Caelia's eyes shone with a flickering, uncertain knowledge.

"He was the British soldier who kidnapped your mother." Clare's expression changed as she gazed off into the distant past. "He...forced Lila in the beginning, but he came to care for her, even to love her. As all men did." Her eyes filled with tears she wasn't aware of. "She escaped from him once and came back to Malcolm, but Kingston could no' let her go. He came for her and caught her when she was out ridin' without an escort. Malcolm was heartbroken. And when she tried to leave the Major-General again, he...killed her. He must've regretted it later, which is why he let her house and crops stand."

The tears began to fall, and for once she could not hide her weakness.

Caelia could only stare in disbelief. "Ye loved him!"

Clare was lost. The effort had taken too much. "Who?

"My father!" it was part accusation, part exclamation, part compassion.

"He loved me too, once. After my family came back from France, while my sister Lila was travellin' with my father, attendin' balls and teas and luncheons. Malcolm and I grew very close. He was ready to ask for my hand when Lila and my father returned home.

"I was a better student than she, who was two years my senior, but she was quick to learn just enough. She was beautiful, with her golden blond hair that fell to her knees when unbound. Like a delicate flower, a butterfly that darted about—full of joy and a sense of adventure and passion. She drew people in her wake; they could no' resist. Like a Chinese shadow dancer, she was seductive, charmin', always laughin' or singin' in her sweet soprano voice. Everyone loved her; everyone wanted her. Malcolm could no' turn her away. No one could. No' even me."

Caelia forgot everything but Clare's pain, etched clearly on her suddenly aging face. "Did she know ye loved him?"

Her aunt gripped the hand her niece offered. She saw the dejection in Caelia's expression. "No. She'd been far away, had she no'? Dancin' with army officers, English and Scots both. How could she know?"

By looking with her eyes open, Caelia guessed silently. If she, Caelia, could see it so clearly all these years later, it must have lit Clare like a lantern back then, like the reflected glow of a full moon. She was bursting with sorrow, compassion and affection for the woman who had raised her—her sister's child with the man she loved—but never said a word, until Caelia had surprised her and pressed her, as the girl had been doing too often recently. She glanced down guiltily at Clare's hand and hers, fingers entwined so tightly that the flesh was white and taut.

"I love ye Ma-clare. More than I've ever told ye."

Clare shook her head violently. "Forgive me for speaking of my grief. Tis no' right. I should be strong and protect ye, no' draw ye inside my own sorrow. Forgive me."

"There's naught to forgive."

"The lies—"

"The lies were to protect me, just as ye said. Mayhap I wish I'd known the truth sooner, but at least I've no' been livin' with a broken heart."

Clare stiffened as her niece's last words intruded on her memories. *What're ye doin', ye fool?* she chided herself silently. *How did this happen?* She made it a point never to feel sorry for herself. She had so much, after all. Even if she did not have the one thing she most wanted. *Weel, the two things. Malcolm's love and Celia's trust.*

Chapter 13

Wandering about the house like the wraith of her dead mother, Caelia tried to reconcile what she had learned with what she already knew. She had heard many times about Lila Rose's beauty and charm; about how she danced through the world, carefree and captivating. She had heard of Clare's love for her sister, and Malcolm's for his wife— but never from her father himself, now that she thought about it. When he spoke Lila's name, he said it softly, and he still wore a thick ruby ring she had given him. Caelia had seen his rooms many times when she was a child, and there was no portrait of Lila above the cherrywood mantel. The only image of Lila Rose she had ever seen was in the pocketwatch in her mother's secret chest.

Her active imagination swam with questions, and she yearned to go down to the loch and swim, or climb one of the nearby mountains until she was too exhausted to think. She wanted to go find Robert and ask him questions she could no longer put to her aunt. Or was it the sweet taste of his lips that kept his face always in the forefront of her mind? It did not matter either way, because she did not know where he was staying, or what his purpose was in coming here, or why he knew so much about her mother. Why was it so important to him that she know the truth? Had anything changed since he'd come to know so much about her? *He does, doesn't he?* she thought. *He knows practically everything.*

Her head was spinning from all the questions without answers. She was on her way downstairs when she heard her father come in. Clare met him in the hallway at the bottom of the stairs. Caelia paused, knowing she should slip back up to her rooms, but she could not make herself move.

Clare was whispering, so she could not hear everything she was saying, but she saw Malcolm Rose's face go pale, then flush with color. "Why didn't ye wait?" he said too loudly.

Caelia shrank back to make certain she could not be seen.

"...had to tell her!" Clare snapped. "...barely think what to say...terrible!"

Brushing the disheveled hair from her cheek, Malcolm said, "I ken, *mo-cridhe*..."

Then Caelia could not hear any more, because he put his hand on Clare's shoulder and guided her into his private office, where a big fire burned, fighting the chill of the overcast spring day.

Mo-cridhe, he had said, and his touch had been tender, but not a lover's touch. Caelia wondered what Clare felt when he touched her thus in friendship.

Turning back up the stairs, Caelia went to the one place where she knew she would always find answers. Clare and Malcolm had long ago forbidden her to sketch or paint them—after she sat with them one Saturday evening, a sketchbook in her lap, and casually drew them in their comfortable rocking chairs as they spoke in low voices before a cheerful fire.

She was humming to herself, so absorbed in her work she did not even hear what they were saying. She raised her head, startled, when her father said with forced pleasantry, "What have ye there, lass?"

She handed him the idyllic scene. Only it wasn't. Both expressions were nearly blank, but a current of anger ran between them. And Clare had two heads: one with the blank stare, one turned away and drawn with grief.

Caelia gaped. She had not yet become used to the truths her paintings revealed. She honestly expected the sketch to be warm and full of affection. "I beg yer pardon," she said hurriedly. "I didn't mean to." She waved her hand distractedly over the offending image. "I just...ye looked so sweet by the fire."

"Did ye hear what we said?" her father asked, attempting to keep his tone even.

"No, I didna."

Aware of her sincerity and distress, the two adults assured her it was not her fault and sent her off to bed, where she should have been in any case. She could not banish from her mind how they stood erect, contained, separate in every way except their united attempt to spare her more pain. She felt sorry for them—so deeply that she ached with it.

Caelia crept away in shame, and was surprised when both came up to kiss her good night. Not until the next morning did they tell her not to draw them anymore.

She swore she would not, had tried to obey, but once she sensed the hurt beneath their cheerful smiles, she'd often tried to draw one or the other when they were not aware. Making quick sketches to capture their features, she worked on the portraits in solitude, trying to figure out what they were really feeling. She hid the drawings and paintings in her studio, where her parents rarely went.

Frustrated, feeling the urgent need to sketch something new from the well of imagination that was driving her, the sensation of the sticks of pastel between her fingers, to see the color and life take shape beneath her hands, it came to her that she needed the glen, the air, freedom from the empathy which thrust her will-she nil-she into the grief of others.

She hurried to her room and changed into her working clothes: a plain blouse and hunter green broadcloth skirt to which she had attached large pockets for holding chalk and blending brushes and the smooth round stones she collected. Leaving her panniers, corset and petticoats in the armoire, she put a box of pastels in her pocket and left by the tower stairs that promised release.

She did not stop until she reached the ferns and trees crowding in beside the River Affric, which she followed to the ruins of a small unknown castle, covered with ivy and bright yellow lichen, climbing roses and honeysuckle. She hiked up her skirt and climbed over the lowest wall. Folding up her red plaid she made a comfortable spot to sit on, held the canvas in her lap, closed her eyes and summoned Robert's face. It came to her at once, half-smiling, half-lit by desire. With all her body and her mind she thought of the long moment when his lips had descended to hers. Her heart fluttered with anticipation, just as it had then. Delightful chills ran through her body when she remembered how he had tilted her face to his, meeting her lips with his warm, moist mouth. She could feel the body heat that lingered inside his coat when he gave it to her to protect her from the rain.

Such feelings were forbidden, she knew, and she had always been a good girl. But Robert's kiss had changed that. Everything he was had changed her. Caelia began to sing her favorite touching ballad from Allan Ramsay's book of songs.

Of race divine thou needs must be,
Since nothing earthly equals thee;
For heaven's sake, oh! favour me,
Who only lives to love thee.

It was as natural to her as breathing. The music caught her up as surely as the whisper of a breeze after the rain.

An thou were my ain thing,
I would love thee, I would love thee:
An thou were my ain thing,
How dearly would I love thee!

Caught her up and carried her away to a world of color and light and imagination as she opened her eyes and saw that she'd been sketching for some time.

She blushed at what she had done. Robert's tall body was naked, though not quite finished, and the wind was tangled in his hair; she could feel it moving there.

So long's I had the use of light,
I'd on thy beauties feast my sight,
Then in soft whispers through the night,
I'd tell how much I lov'd thee.

An thou were my ain thing,
I would love thee....

She wondered if he could hear her song. She sang all the many verses, letting inspiration carry the pastels she held with her thumb and two fingers. *Caelia, I can't promise*—he had begun, but she had silenced him. For once she did not want to talk. She wanted to feel, to give herself up to sensation as she was doing now.

My passion, constant as the sun,
Flames stronger still, will ne'er have done
Till fates my threads of life have spun.
Which breathing out, I'll love thee.

She could smell the damp grasses and ferns, and the water rising from the river. She could smell the peaty bank and the Caledonia pines spread through the forest and climbing up the distant mountainsides. She could taste the moisture in the air, and the sweet honeysuckle, and the smile on her lips.

An thou were my ain thing,
I would love thee, I would love thee:
An thou were my ain thing,
How dearly would I love thee!

The river rushed past, swirling over the great stones that formed its banks and the small stones its bottom. It sang its own song in tune with the sighing wind, and in that blessed harmony, Caelia forgot everything but tactile sensation and the deep, beguiling hues that seduced her, along with the memory of Robert's face. She was full of joy; she was creating; she was lost altogether and thrilled to be so.

While love does at his alter stand,
Have thee my heart, give me thy hand,
And with your smile thou shalt command
The will of him who loves thee.

When the last of her songs finally ended, and wind grew still and expectant, the water murmured, *Show it, look into it, consume it*. She shook her head to clear it, then held the portrait out to see what she had created.

Caelia gasped and dropped the canvas into the tangle of vines at her feet. Robert was there; it was definitely him in every line and shading and stroke of pastel. He stood tall and proud, strong and determined in the uniform she had come to know well, though she had never seen a man wearing one. She stared and stared at the gold braid, the brass buttons, the knee-length red coat, white breeches and tall shiny boots. A British military uniform. She remembered then how he had reached out to stop her as she slipped her hand into his coat pocket. How he'd answered too quickly that he found the button in the road, though she was barely interested. His strange expression when she mentioned how shiny it was, and he told her he'd shined it up. She hadn't been paying attention then; her mind was crowded with other thoughts and feelings.

Now she could not look away. The buttons on his tunic exactly matched the one she'd held in her palm earlier that day. He'd lied to her about a thing so simple that it took her breath away. He was an English soldier. Perhaps he was not Scottish at all. Her heart pounded, raced, ached at a new, sharp pain. "He's a spy," she said to the ancient stones of the tower, to the ivy that had covered and devoured them. "An English spy."

She was silent for a moment, then started to laugh. "Like my mother." She laughed so hard that tears ran down her cheeks. "He's just exactly like my mother!"

Chapter 14

Robert Hamilton put down the dispatch from the general, asking for information regarding Caelia Rose. His throat felt tight with guilt, and a wave of protectiveness swept over him. She was his assignment, but he did not want to hurt her any more than he already had. He stared at his face in the mirror and remembered her dexterous fingers moving across the canvas, the vivid jade pastel leaving a pattern of curves that hinted at a pulsating green ocean.

He tugged at his hair in frustration. Things had changed for him today: for both of them. It was not as though he wanted to give up on making her see the truth. How could she ever become a woman with a woman's understanding if she did not know exactly who and what she had come from? But he no longer cared about his secret orders. He suspected he never really had. He had come out of fierce curiosity and little else. Lila Rose had drawn him here, into the heart of her daughter's life, as surely as if her ghost had appeared and refused to go until he followed her commands.

Lila the beautiful. Lila the enthralling. Lila who'd been everything a daughter should never be.

In that instant, Robert knew what he had to do. He had to talk to Caelia. Now. To tell her—could he tell her everything? No, because part of it was not his story to tell. All he knew was he could not risk losing her. Not ever.

Taking up his frockcoat from the chairback where it had recently stopped steaming near the fire, he swung it over his shoulders and fastened the buttons in the front. "Caelia, *mo-charaid*," he said out loud, "I'm on my way."

~ * ~

Suddenly it was all too much to bear, and Caelia could not stop the tears. She hated weeping, yet seemed to be doing it far too often lately. She willed herself to stop, but just then her grief was stronger than her will.

She could not look away from the painting. She had learned, through the years, that everything she painted was true in a sense that frightened her with the intensity of its meaning. Indisputably True. She had told Robert she wasn't a seer, but deep inside she knew it was a lie. Somehow, for reasons she could never begin to understand, she had been born with the gift—if gift it was—of knowing things beyond her ken. But only when she painted. She did not 'see' things in her everyday life, or sense things, or feel darkness coming. Sometimes her dreams felt like premonitions, but they only became real if she got up and made a sketch or a full-scale painting. Like the one she had done of Glen Affric, beautiful and peaceful in its stillness until Robert Hamilton's shadow covered the ground, breaking the spell.

And now this. A British soldier. Fatal enemy of Jacobites and Highlanders alike. No wonder he became angry so easily. No wonder he kept so many secrets. But why, *why*, WHY had he come? What did he want from her? *Are ye sure yer mother was a spy for the Jacobites?*

What had her father said? *He made her tell him everything she knew, that cruel major-general. But that doesn't diminish what she did for us.*

She'd answered him in her steadiest voice. *Of course it does. It means she was no' the woman I thought she was. It means she was a coward and a traitor.*

The English would have called her a traitor anyway. "Aye, so they would," she whispered into Robert's painted face.

She thought back to the very first day, when her aunt

had warned, *I've asked ye before no' to wear yer plaid, but to hide it away. If anyone should see ye, ye could be fined or sent to prison."*

Naively, Caelia had replied, *My friends will no' tell.* And Clare, wise, careful Clare said, *Mayhap no' yer friends, but what of the stranger?* The stranger, the soldier, the enemy of all things from the Highland past.

I feel like a fool, like ye thought twould break me, like ye think of me still as a child. She did not know why Robert Hamilton had come or why it helped this stranger to destroy her faith in her mother. She had no idea who he really was.

But one thing she knew for certain. She was not a child anymore. Today she had become a woman. The tears had stopped falling and she swore they would not come again.

Chapter 15

The mist was fine as it drifted upward from the roots of the trees and the loch and the fuming river. Caelia was grateful; its touch felt like a benediction, though it did not ease her stinging soul. She was headed back to her room to hide the painting in a corner. She did not want to see it again, and was not sure she should show it to her aunt and father. But she could not bring herself to toss it away with the garbage in the stableyard. She wanted to, to show what she thought of this Truth, to prove to the Gods that she did not want the gift any longer. Except she could not do it. Her arm would not move—literally.

She had reached the bottom of the hill when she heard a voice through the thickening mist.

"Caelia, is that ye?"

She knew that voice. She hurried her step.

"Please. I need to speak to ye."

She kept walking, deciding at the last minute to take the obvious path to the front door so he wouldn't see the one that led to the tower. That must remain her secret. Especially from him.

"I beg ye, lass. Tis important."

She could not see him yet, and was determined not to look, although the mere sound of his voice brought back emotions and sensations she would rather forget. She shuddered and forged ahead.

Then he was upon her. Of course he was. She walked the glen daily, climbed up and down the river, swam in the lake, and climbed the lower mountains—now blue-gray in the distance. She was strong and fit, but he was a soldier. She remembered now, though she did not think she had noticed before, the muscles in his calves and thighs, accented by his soft breeches. The strength in his arms as he held her and brought his lips down to hers. He was stronger, more fit, more ready. He had been trained to run and climb and persevere, trained to stalk his enemies.

She was surprised when he caught up to her that he was out of breath. She continued on her chosen path.

"What is't, my lovely lass? Why will ye no' look at me? Ye were happy when we parted."

She pressed her lips together and remained silent.

Frowning, he stood in front of her to stop her progress. "Caelia?" Realizing that she was not going to respond, he cleared his throat. "I have to confess. To explain—"

"This?" She swung the painting face out.

He stopped, mouth open. He'd been told she was a seer. Why had he not listened? "No, no' that. But I've no choice now, have I?"

"I don't care, Mr. Hamilton. Or should I call ye by yer rank?"

"Ye'd never have spoken to me if I'd told ye. I could no' risk that."

She blinked in astonishment. "I suppose no'. Because ye've a reason for bein' here, and tis all for ye, and no' for me at all. I came to believe ye cared about me a wee bit, but I see I was as much a fool with ye as I was with my parents. Everyone lies, it seems."

All he could do was stare. She seemed somewhat taller, and her voice was certainly more resolute and controlled. She was different from the girl he'd set out with to find the cave this morning, and not just because of the kiss. He wished with all his heart that was what had changed her, but he could see it went much deeper.

"I would have told ye," he said quietly, "just no' quite yet."

"Because ye knew I'd hate ye for it." She took a short breath, then added, "How long have ye been a soldier for the Crown?"

All at once he realized she had control, not he, and somewhere within his despair he was proud of her strength in this moment. He had the good grace to stare down at his shoes. "Since I was 17."

Caelia swallowed dryly. "So ye've made it yer life's work, then."

He'd never thought it could sound so ugly. "No...aye, but tis no' what ye think."

"I'd no' see how it could be otherwise. Ye're a soldier with allegiance to an army that tried to destroy us. Isn't it so?"

"Aye, but ye must let me explain."

"Why? Ye're no' very good at explainin' or answerin' questions. Ye seem to like askin' them much more." Her stomach clenched and she was overwhelmed by how true her accusations were. She felt his treachery like a fresh wound.

"But don't ye see, I'm still the man I was this mornin'." His hazel eyes were pleading, as if he actually cared what she thought of him.

Caelia felt the mist was settling in her throat. The glen she loved was suddenly strange and uncomfortable. "Aye, so ye are. A spy for the English." Bitterness filled her voice. It deepened when, for the first time, her rage faded and she realized she wanted to forget the painting, forget the truth, and tell him what she'd learned from Clare. She'd talked to him as she talked to no one else. He'd told her truths her own parents had hidden from her. She would miss him, and though she'd only felt them once, she would miss his arms around her. And his kisses. Because she simply could not let him stay. This was too much—too huge a betrayal. He knew how she felt about the British, especially the army.

"No, never! Tis the other way around." He was afraid she wouldn't let him finish, so he hurried on. "I'm a Scot who joined the army to keep watch for Scotland and the

Highlands, which I love more than my life. Ever since I was a lad, I've made myself indispensible to the British, and dedicated myself to helping the Scots."

Staring at him in disbelief, she shook her head slowly. "*Our* spy, are ye? Then why did ye no' tell me?"

"Because no one livin' knows. I could no' take the risk of tellin'."

Her expression was blank and chilly. She didn't believe him. How could she?

"Caelia, *mo-charaid*, I didn't understand until today that much as I love the Highlands and my country, I love ye more. I came here to tell ye that." She looked away for a long moment and he began to hope. Surely her hesitation meant she was reconsidering.

When she finally looked up, her face was etched with confusion and bitterness. Her eyes were completely golden, like the eyes of wildcat protecting her cub, except her cub was her own breaking heart. "No," she said, "now I can't take the risk. Tis too late and too painful and I've no one left to believe in!"

She ran then, because she could not bear to stand a moment longer in his presence.

"There are still things ye must know," he said quietly to her retreating back.

She'll no' listen to me, Robert Hamilton thought. *Mayhap she can no' hear me even if she would. I waited too long.* He waited until the door to the manor house closed behind her with a final crack, and then he turned away, though every instinct, every muscle, cried out for him to stay.

Chapter 16

The door swung closed behind Caelia and she leaned against it, exhausted and in torment. Her hands were shaking and her heart pounded all the way up to her head, where her sorrow became a throbbing pain. She was out of breath, though she had not been running, as if she had held it in to keep from feeling the weight in her chest. Yet the weight grew heavier with every moment. But she did not weep. It hurt too much to dare.

"Did I hear the door?" Malcolm Rose came out of the morning room in only his shirt and trews, and the deerskin slippers he wore inside the house, where the high stone walls and drafty ceilings insured the rooms were rarely warm enough. "Ah, Caelia. At last. Clare and I have spoken at length, and we've agreed—" He broke off when he took in her disheveled state, her glazed expression that could not hide the pain beneath. Then he noticed the painting she had forgotten to hide from him as she usually did. Robert Hamilton a soldier for the Crown? Whatever Malcolm had expected from the mysterious stranger, it had not been that.

What disturbed him most, however, was his daughter's obvious distress. When had this young man come to matter so much?

Malcolm pressed his eyes closed, trying to gain extra courage. An instant later he opened them and went to Caelia.

"What ails ye, *mo-run*?" When he touched her shoulder, he was shocked to feel how cold she was, even through the red Rose plaid. "Come, have some tea and brandy and sit by the fire." Unobtrusively, he set the painting aside and guided her to the open door of the morning room, where a healthy fire burned.

Caelia was aware that she was sitting suddenly, staring
out the wide windows at the luminous evening light that
fused the starflowers and celandine and bluebells with the
yellow and green grasses, so they looked like an artist's
fine strokes across the canvas of the glen. For once the
beauty did not charm her. She was empty now, numb.

When Malcolm poured tea with a generous portion of
brandy for them both, she noticed how he seemed
monochromatic in his ivory shirt, off-white trews, his sandy
hair and pallid face. She felt she was meant to ask him
something, but couldn't think what it was.

She breathed slowly past the constriction in her throat,
taking a sip of hot tea that burned its way down through her
body, thawing the center but nothing else.

Her father waited till she had drunk it all, then put the
mug aside. "I saw the paintin', lass. We knew we could no'
trust the man."

"Ye were right. Rude men, all-knowin' men, deceivin'
men. He came here to spy on us, I know it."

Malcolm leaned back in his chair. "Did he now? What
for, might I ask? There's no one cares much what we do
anymore, so long as we don't make trouble."

Surely her father was not defending Robert Hamilton?
"But why else would he come?" Her tone was shriller than
she intended. She forced herself to sound calm. "Knowin'
so much about us as he does."

Caelia had never thought of her father as old, but he
looked it just then. His usually suntanned cheeks were pale,
and there were new lines around his eyes and mouth. If she
were not mistaken, they'd come on Robert Hamilton's
heels. "Everything was good before he came, but he's
ruined it. For all of us."

Her father heard things in her voice that made him
wince. It came to him like the ray of light caressing his
knee at that instant, that he no longer knew his daughter.
"Twas no' exactly good, lass. We tried to tell ourselves

twas, tried hard to believe it, but there were always these secrets holdin' us back." Staring into his own tea, Malcolm seemed to come to a decision. "I'd not be knowin' what he hoped to accomplish, but from what I've seen, that young man came because of yer mother. Because he wanted ye to know the truth."

"I don't care about the truth. I just want my family back!"

He was beside her in a second, holding her in his arms, rocking her as she shuddered against his shoulder. "Ye've no' lost us. That will never happen. Never! Ye're what holds us together, ye must know that. We love ye, both of us, so verra much."

Clinging to him as she had not done since she was much younger, Caelia felt his strength seeping into her, his sensible and straightforward approach to life. She'd always loved him for that—for providing the certainty and stability that contrasted so sharply with what she knew of her mother. From the beginning, he made her feel safe and she was grateful, because, with her 'gift' she was never sure, never constant: things were always unpredictable. "I know ye do," she murmured. "And I ye."

He tensed and she felt a change, as if she should be comforting him, rather than the other way around, though she could not imagine why. For a while longer they sat together, his cheek resting on top of her head, and took in each other's warmth.

Finally, Malcolm returned to his highback chair, sat up ramrod straight and began, "Now as I mentioned when ye came in, Clare and I have been talkin', and tis time to tell ye Clare's part of the story about Lila." Back still rigid, he stared at his slippered feet intently. "Ye see, yer mother was the reason Clare became a real Jacobite spy—a *true* hero."

"More spies?" Caelia felt laughter bubbling up but could not let it take hold. She knew it would lead to hysterical tears. "Mayhap I've had enough of spies for one day—or a lifetime."

Her father patted her leg absently. "Aye, so it seems. But tis time to stop the lies now, lass. Time ye knew what there is to know."

She cursed Robert Hamilton under her breath for ever having set foot in Glen Affric. But just as it was too late for them, it was too late to avoid the answers she'd been searching for all along.

Chapter 17

"I'm thinkin' of the letters ye found in yer mother's chest. Ye've read them, aye?"

Caelia blinked at him in shock. "How did ye know—?"

He smiled crookedly. "Of course we knew exactly what was in that chest we gave ye. Even the small hidden one. We wanted ye to discover her on yer own."

It had been a delightful journey, unearthing the lovely carved box and coming to know its contents by heart. Her little secret—an adventure she would never forget. Malcolm and Clare had given her that, since they could not give her Lila. Her chest throbbed with pain of another kind. "I thank ye for that."

"Aye, weel…" For some reason he looked sadder than before.

Caelia went to sit at his feet and laid her head on his knee. "Tell me, Papa."

Absently he petted her hair and seemed to find comfort in the motion. "So ye've read the letters and know yer mother wrote to her sister sometimes over the years. What ye don't know is how often Clare wrote to Lila, giving her advice and love and care. She felt responsible for her."

"Aye, so she said." Caelia had memorized the letters, and the words came easily to mind.

Clare, my dearest, I miss ye so. I'm confused by all the intrigue and treachery. I love the adventure, you know I do, but how do I know who to trust? You would know if you were here. Please come join me and help me think straight.

She had not read Clare's letters, but knowing her aunt as she did, and all the sound practical, compassionate advice she's given her niece over the years, Caelia was sure she had been even more generous with her sister, before she lost Lila and her world was torn apart.

"Lila leaned on her, though she never followed Clare's advice."

Oh Clare! I know you say I should not risk notoriety by my behavior, but oh! the handsome men I've danced with, and the secrets they've told me! I love to dance above all else, and to kiss mysterious men in the moonlight! I've carried so many messages for Papa, and no one suspects me, because I dance and smile and kiss! How glad I am not to be stuck with you at home!!!

Even when Caelia had read it the first time, she'd been a bit uneasy at the last line, but she'd been under Lila Rose's spell, and hadn't wanted to see anything negative. But now it was clear. "Go on," she urged her father.

"When she was…taken by the major-general…"

The sound of his voice faded out as the sound of her mother's on paper became urgently real.

Help me, Clare! A Major-General has kidnapped me. Every night he takes me brutally. He moves his soldiers relentlessly, so I don't know where I'll be. Get me away from him, I beg you!

Few others had followed, and when they did, they were scribbled on scraps of paper; Lila had obviously been in a hurry. They told of her misery, and after she escaped that once and came home to the Hill o' the Hounds, then was recaptured, his mistreatment when he discovered her pregnancy. Caelia had winced when she read those last; her mother was far too good at describing her suffering.

"Tis when Clare decided to join the rebels in body as well as in spirit," Malcolm said in a weary tone.

His daughter looked up at that, at the exhaustion in his face—too old for his 45 years—his hands pressed palm to palm between his knees, the way he leaned forward, as if a great weight lay upon his shoulders.

"She began to track the movement of guns and willing Highland soldiers, and the British from place to place, following Prince Charles's army and carrying messages about what she'd learned, hoping to hear news of Lila or the major-general. First she had to learn which major-general he was, and that took tricky maneuvering on her part. Then, once she discovered it was Kingston, one of five main British commanders in Scotland, it was a bit easier. But every question she asked put her at risk. Her curiosity had to appear to be about all of them at once, or her life might have been forfeit."

Appalled by his gray, pallid skin, Caelia reached for him. "Papa!"

But he did not seem to hear her. "She was in incredible danger every moment, crossing British lines when she thought Kingston might be in the area. She had to try to infiltrate his private quarters. But fortunately she never got close enough. She heard rumors that her sister was a traitor, that she had told the major-general all she knew about Prince Charles Edward and his plans, but Clare knew how mistrustful the Highlanders were, and paid their doubts no mind. She would not believe ill of Lila. That was her mistake. And mine."

You must come to me in his tent, for he keeps me with him always. I cannot bear this any longer. Come at once, Clare. Hurry!

Caelia had always thought Lila's faith in her sister was touching, but now it began to sound a bit selfish. And why had she not written to her husband, who was far better equipped to rescue her from the vicious major-general?

Kathryn Lynn Davis

Why was there no mention at all of Malcolm Rose? Chills rose along her arms and slithered down her back. All at once she did not want to listen.

He took a deep shuddering breath. His daughter was afraid to interrupt him.

"When your aunt finally reached that elusive British camp, she discovered, to her horror, that Lila had been lying to her all along. The suspicious Jacobites had been right. She saw other things to terrible to repeat. Such sufferin' and death and betrayal. And Lila at its heart."

Caelia realized she wasn't breathing, but did not know how to begin once more. Finally she exhaled in a painful burst and asked, "Where's Clare?"

"She could no' tell ye this, or be here when ye heard. She said to apologize to ye for her weakness."

Rising impatiently, Caelia began to pace. "No. Clare's the most powerful woman I've ever known. But she loved her sister so much. When she learned the truth it must've destroyed her, and ye." She turned to see her father had tears in his eyes.

"Verra nearly, lass. But we had ye to think of, and that gave us strength."

"And ye didn't tell me this because…" She trailed off, watching him intently.

"Because there was no point. Why should we shatter yer dreams of yer mother when she was dead and gone? Ye had little enough, livin' here alone with us. We could at least give ye that."

"Oh, Papa!" she cried, crouching beside him and hugging him tightly. "Ye gave me everything I ever wanted."

"Weel," he murmured into her mass of light brown hair, "weel now. I've only told ye now because of Mr. Hamilton and his questions. Twas time."

She leaned back on her heels, disconcerted. "Aye," she said at last, "ye're right."

"But Caelia?" His blue eyes were pleading.
"What is it, Papa?" she asked, alarmed.
He looked away. "Nothing, *mo-run*. Nothing at all."

Chapter 18

Having barely made it up the stairs, dizzy with the day's many revelations, Caelia sat on her bed and tried not to think, but to no avail. Thoughts and images circled in her mind and kept her from resting: her mother in Kingston's arms; Clare hiding in the woods as British soldiers passed, bayonetted rifles at the ready; Robert pleading with Caelia to listen; and her father when she'd kissed his cheek and hugged him before she came up. She couldn't understand why he looked so defeated.

She ached desperately, but not in her body—rather in her bewildered soul. Nothing was as she'd supposed: not the mother she'd worshipped or the aunt she loved or the man she'd accidentally come to care for. Not even her father, who felt somehow like a stranger in that warm room she'd always loved.

Unconsciously she picked up a sketchbook and black pastel that lay on her bedside table. She could always disappear into the world of art and images. She began to draw leisurely, singing to herself.

When she woke from the trance the song had lured her into, she saw that she'd drawn Robert again. This time he was much more casually dressed than he usually was. He didn't look the least bit like a military man. He was ordinary, yet not at all ordinary. Every muscle in his body was taut with purpose; his eyes shone, and his face glowed with a passion she recognized. She saw it whenever she looked into her silver gilt mirror, which was only when she was sketching or painting. It was what she felt for her art and for her family. What was it for him?

She thought about Clare's story, how she'd been tricked into becoming a spy. *When Lila was taken by the major-general…tis when Clare decided to join the rebels in body as well as in spirit.* And Robert had told her, *Ever since I was a lad, I've made myself indispensible to the British, and dedicated myself to helping the Scots.* It could be true. Everyone had different motives. She realized she wanted to believe him. She could not rest with the thoughts and voices ringing in her head.

"Caelia?"

She looked up, startled to see Clare standing hesitantly on the threshold. Clare was never hesitant; she always knew exactly what to do and say and think. Though recently that had changed.

"May I?"

"Of course ye may. Come in." Caelia was disturbed by her aunt's reticence and pitied Clare in a way she did not wish to. Her aunt had always been the stalwart one, the imperturbable and self-possessed woman Caelia turned to when she needed help and knowledge and strength. For consolation, cheer and hope, she had gone to her father. And to both of them for love. Now, all at once, they seemed to be looking to her for comfort.

She moved over on the bed and her aunt sat across from her, legs crossed beneath her ample skirts. She was wearing a new gown in pale grey silk, the bodice, sleeves and hem embroidered with tiny bluebells. "Tis beautiful," Caelia observed, running her fingers across the intricate embroidery. "It makes yer eyes shine." Her gray-blue eyes did glitter in the light through the huge windows. The gown contrasted sharply with Caelia's plain muslin blouse and stomacher above a worn hunter green skirt.

"I doubt if tis the gown, lass." Clare took her niece's hands, staring down at them for a short time. "I came to beg yer pardon for no' tellin' ye the truth sooner."

"Mayhap I was no' ready to hear it sooner—or at all."

Clare half-smiled. "No, ye were right when ye pointed out ye're no longer a child. We'd no wish to believe ye,

Malcolm and I. Twas easier when ye were a bairn and yer questions were all about fairies and magic and color and paint. Those we could answer happily by hurtin' no one. But once ye become a woman, things are different, more complicated." She was moved when her niece squeezed her hands with affection and a kind of recognition.

"Ye must understand, lass. I loved my sister fiercely, protectively, as a mother loves her child—for our mother lived in a world of her own, believing money would be enough to take care of her daughters. I was halfway pretty and intelligent and caring, but I was no' a butterfly; I was no' enchanted. I was a woman, not the shadow of an unearthly glow too beautiful to be real. Everyone believed Lila was as worldly as she was seductive, as wise as she was alluring, as prepared for adventure as she lived and yearned for it. But I knew better. And I swore to protect my fragile butterfly."

Sighing, she continued. "She left behind many broken hearts when my family left France to return to Scotland, where our father had been born. He came back because he knew the time was coming for Scotland's king to return to the throne of England. For James II's grandson to come and make the Highlands and all of Britain right again. Time for a revolution.

"Maman was bored with it all and fled back to France. I believed James to be the true king, but I was apprehensive, thinkin' of the times the Jacobites had failed before."

"And wise ye were." Caelia nodded.

"But Lila? Lila was thrilled. *A revolution*, she sang as she danced through the house on her toes. *My adventure has come at last*. And then Father took her away with him, introducing her as if she were part of his Jacobite plan. She didn't realize, just didn't know what the cost would be, Caelia, *mo-cridhe*."

"But ye knew," her niece said with a trace of venom,

"and ye're the one who paid the price."

"She…gave her life," Clare managed.

"So did ye."

Clare could not argue with that. "I never believed in fairies, but I wanted ye to for as long as possible. To believe in your mother as weel, like a magical being who dwelt in another realm. To believe and be content."

"I've been more than content, Ma-Clare. I love being with ye and Papa, ye know I do, and here in the glen, and the thrill of creatin'. All these things have filled my heart to burstin'."

"And now?"

"Now none of them have changed—only what I know of Lila Rose. Mayhap she's made my heart just a bit less full." Gazing at her aunt's familiar face, Caelia decided she could be strong for her if that's what she needed. For all the times when she'd felt she was losing her footing, and Clare had reached out to help her stand on firm ground again. "Mayhap I've occupied my mind with other things, because tis easier that way."

"Things like him?" Clare nodded toward the black and white sketch her niece had forgotten to hide. She had seen the painting leaning against the wall when she came in, but did not remark upon it. But it angered her, just as it had angered Caelia. Until she saw the simple sketch in her niece's lap.

Staring at the French duvet, Caelia tried to think what to say. All that came out was, "Aye."

"Have ye seen him since?" Clare indicated the painting of Robert in uniform.

"Aye." Caelia could not decide whether she was embarrassed, ashamed or angry.

"What did he say?"

There was no hint of judgment in her aunt's tone, which surprised her. "He said he was a Scot who joined the army to keep watch for Scotland and the Highlands. Said he loved them more than his life," she repeated, wondering if it would sound truer now than it had then.

"Do ye believe him?" Clare asked, again without judgment, though she had reason enough to dislike him.

"I want to believe him, but don't quite know how." *Ever since I was a lad, I've made myself indispensible to the British, and dedicated myself to helping the Scots.* "And anyway, he lied to me." A fresh wash of anger tinged with pain rushed through her.

"We lied to ye, *mo-run.* Do ye blame us?"

"No! I've told ye I love ye. Ye were only tryin' to protect me."

Clare's smile was soft and full of hope. "Tis really how ye feel?"

Caelia leaned forward and hugged her. "Aye, tis."

"Then consider this. What was Robert Hamilton tryin' to do?"

Chewing her lip, Caelia realized there was only one answer. "To make ye tell me the truth. He said twas time I knew."

"He was right, was he no'?"

"I dinna ken how, but aye, he was right." *But don't ye see, I'm still the man I was this mornin'.* "It doesn't matter, don't ye see? How can I trust him?

She pulled away, tossing the sketchbook aside.

"Oh, aye? Mayhap ye're only lookin' for a reason no' to trust. Mayhap ye're really afraid."

Caelia tensed. "I'm no' afraid of anythin'!"

Regarding her niece sympathetically, Clare whispered, "Mayhap ye're no frightened of Himself, but of the things he makes ye feel."

Caelia deflated like a set of silk skirts when the whalebone hoops are removed. "I thought ye'd no likin' for him?"

Clare's eyes filled with tears she tried hard to blink away. "Tis no matter what I feel. Tis yer feelins we're discussin'. I've felt them all myself, lass, and I know tis near impossible to turn away. I just don't want ye thinkin' ye're wrapped up in anger and doubt, when mayhap ye're in love instead. I never got the chance to follow my heart. Mayhap ye'll tell me what tis like." She left the room before her common sense could make her change her mind.

Caelia was astounded, speechless. She could not believe what was happening. Only this morning Robert had shown her the fairies' cave she had longed all her life to discover; he had kissed her and made her forget the wonders of that magic place; she had learned more about her mother than she ever wanted to know, discovered Robert was not what he seemed, learned her parents were as human as she, and now her aunt seemed to be sending her out into Robert's arms. Yet outside the glen was just inching toward gloaming. She did not know how she would survive the day.

Chapter 19

As Caelia made her way down the tower stairs, she heard a *cuiseach* (a hollow reed whistle) playing a haunting tune that called to her as the river called, as the singing wind called, as the words of the ancients—the *Tuatha de Dannan*—called. She could not resist it any more than she could resist the lilac tint of gloaming or the sound of Robert's voice, *Caelia,* mo-charaid, *I didn't understand until today that, much as I love the Highlands and my country, I love ye more.* When had he said that? She had not heard it before. Or had she? Had she been so consumed with bitterness that she had not listened? But now the words would not be silent. They wove themselves among the silver notes of the mystical song of the *cuiseach*, tempting her, moving her, singing in her heart.

The glen was still and waiting, as it often was at gloaming, in those enchanted hours that were neither day nor night, when the trees were drenched in violet mist. The cotton grass swayed as Caelia crossed lightly, leaving her footsteps in soft indentations behind her.

And then she saw his silhouette on a brae beside the loch. He held a *cuiseach* to his lips, blowing the tune that summoned her, drawing her toward him as inexorably as the night drew the sun toward its rest. Her pulse throbbed in her ears and her vision blurred. Her hands trembled, and that made her angry. She was not the weak and innocent girl he thought her. She refused to be! Yet the closer she got, the more erratic her heartbeat, leaving her breathless when he finally turned and saw her.

"Caelia?" His question was not about who she was, but why she was there.

"Aye." She stopped a few arm-lengths away, flushed

and tentative.

Robert was elated but wary. She was still out of reach, but at least she was here. "Will ye let me explain now?"

"Ye did that already. I just wasn't listenin'."

"And now?" He could not help it; he was giddy with hope.

She took a step closer. "Why did ye no' leave the glen?"

He was taken unaware. "I tried, lass, but I could no' leave ye, no matter what ye thought of me."

"And I could no' stay away, no matter what I feared." Caelia's heartbeat did not settle back to normal, but rather pounded furiously. She twined her fingers together to keep her hands still. "Ye never actually lied, except about the button. Twas such a silly thing, that."

She was making excuses for him. Robert did not know whether to smile or grimace. All he knew was that he wanted her to come to him willingly, to trust him that much. He also wanted to touch her reddened cheeks, to cool the flush there and start another, different fire. Her light brown braid was coming loose, and he wanted to remove the wilted ribbon and set the thick locks free.

Drawing her red plaid close to keep out the evening chill, Caelia felt the urge to run and hide. But hadn't she been doing that all her life without even knowing? Hadn't Robert Hamilton taught her that? *That's no reason to stay with him,* an inner voice chided her. *There are other reasons,* she replied silently, surprising herself.

He came off the brae slowly so as not to startle her. She closed the rest of the space between them.

Caelia put out her hand, but whether to stop him or draw him nearer she could not say. She rested it on his chest, stunned at the heat that slight touch sent through her. "I don't know if I trust ye completely," she said as a last attempt at resistance.

"Does it matter, *mo-aghray*?" He pulled her near until

they were a breath apart.

Shivering at the heat of his hands through her garments, Caelia swayed forward. "No' now."

Overwhelmed by pent up anxiety and need, Robert closed his arms around her tightly, then lowered his mouth to hers, kissing her fiercely, feeling the cool gloaming on her soft pink lips. Soon the chill was gone, replaced by the warmth of her desire, which flowed through her young body in tremors of pleasure.

Caelia had never felt the like before. Her lips opened beneath his, ardor meeting ardor, need meeting need. When he drew away and kissed the hollow of her throat, she sighed and leaned her head back. Gently, leisurely, he strung kisses along her cheeks, her forehead, her chin, and back to her neck, which he traced with the tip of his tongue.

She clung to him, sliding her hands up his back to the muscles flexed by their meeting. She explored his broad shoulders, honed by his training, and back down to his waist. She wanted to touch his skin but did not dare. Her mind was whirling with colors so vivid they caught her up and heightened every inch where he caressed her with his soldier's hands, which taught her feelings she could never have imagined.

"Come," Robert whispered, his breath against her ear.

She looked up, met his eyes and nodded.

Without another word, they moved to the soft, giving grass on the far side of the brae. Robert took off his greatcoat and laid it down. Caelia offered her plaid and he took it to make their little nest more comfortable. He made certain no one was about, but the gloaming came late in Scotland, and at this time of the evening, they were all at home in their beds, ready to rise with the dawn.

With great care and tenderness, Robert wrapped the plaid around them, and they lay still in each other's arms for a long while. He watched her face as it revealed every sensation, every thought and every feeling. It frightened him a little, how transparent she was, how easily read. But it also heartened him. It had been a long time since he'd known exactly what someone else was thinking, since he'd trusted someone absolutely the way he trusted her.

"Ye're beautiful, my Caelia," Robert crooned, unknotting the ribbon and freeing her luxuriant hair. It was shiny and oh, so soft, just as he'd expected it to be. He brought it to his nose, the fragrance of honeysuckle wafting past as he took in a deep breath. "So very beautiful." *So different from other women, so open and wondering with yer golden eyes, still the eyes of a wildcat, but full of hunger now instead of rage.*

He let her hair slip through his fingers a few strands at a time, so it settled with a whisper around her softly smiling face—a shimmering crown of curls turned russet by the twilight. He held his body apart from hers, taut with desire so intense it took his breath away. He did not wish to hurry. Not now. Not with Celia. "Do ye love me, *mo-charaid*?" he murmured, shaken because the answer mattered so much.

Caelia felt so many things as he knelt beside her, cupping her face in his palms as if it were sacred; running his fingers through her hair and igniting a tingling warmth that began in each strand and traveled throughout her body; abandoning his self-possessed, observant self to the man with the shining hazel eyes—more green now than brown. The man who could not hide his longing, who, by revealing his need and tenderness and affection, had revealed every last secret he had ever thought to hide.

When she did not answer his question at once, he paused with his hand on the skin at the neck of her pale muslin blouse. "Caelia? Do ye? Love me?"

"I think so, but I dinna ken how to be in love. Ye'll have to show me."

Sitting back on his heels, Robert swallowed dryly. He took her hands in his. "I'd no' be knowin' either. We'll have to learn together." He thought of the lasses of all ages who had made his heart race and his face flush since he'd been a boy. The ones who had taught him how to be a man, and those who had shared their secrets of how to treat a woman. He thought of his infatuations and his passions and the ones he'd surely loved. Except he knew now that he hadn't. He barely knew the woman lying wrapped in a red plaid beside him, yet he knew everything about her and more. Most of all, he knew he could not live without her.

Robert Hamilton lifted Caelia Rose into his arms. She went willingly, offering her lips to his seeking mouth. This time, when her breasts brushed his chest, she knew she wanted more. She began to work his shirt open with shaking fingers.

His slipped his hands under muslin to touch her skin lightly, circling, circling upward.

"Robert!" she cried as her body responded, as the heat curled within her, wilder and fiercer. "I want— I need—"

"I know, my love. I ken."

They stretched out, body to body, yearning to yearning, exaltation to exaltation.

Chapter 20

When they lay still again, and the kaleidoscope of colors in her mind had ceased its magic shifting hues, Caelia curled her head into Robert's shoulder and began to cry. Very quickly her tears became harsh sobs and soon she was fighting for breath.

Robert held her tight, the plaid pulled around them. He rubbed her back in slow, soothing circles, murmuring endearments and soft words of comfort. "What is't, lass? Please tell me. Are ye afraid of what we've done, because I swear I'll never leave ye."

She did not seem to hear him and he felt her tears on his chest long after the shuddering sobs had stopped.

"Please, *mo-aghray*, tell me what ails ye. Even if tis something I've no wish to hear." He caressed her hair, combing his fingers through the tangled mane, trying to restore some order there at least.

She threw her arms around him and held him so close that she set his ribs aching, but he made no complaint. He was becoming desperate. All he wanted was to know how to fix this, though if she regretted their union and wanted him to go, he did not know what he would do. He wanted to ease her pain; it was tearing straight through his heart to hear her so troubled. Helpless in the face of her grief, he realized all his training, his expertise with weapons, his limber body and strong muscles were useless. Nothing had prepared him for this moment.

Finally the tears stopped. Robert used the edge of the red Rose plaid to gently wipe away her tears, and to give her a dry place to rest her head on his chest. But she sat up, looking down into his face with its chiseled chin and cheekbones and the long dark brown hairs curling around it in the misted evening. The plaid fell off her shoulders, exposing them and the top of her breasts to the half-light of the rising moon.

"Twas no' ye—or this." She touched her breast, then the curls on his chest.

She still seemed completely bereft, and he wanted to hold her and rock her until the feeling went away. Except that wasn't what she needed. "Then what? Can ye tell me?"

"Tis just..." her eyes filled again. "For my mam. I know she was a stranger, but I thought I knew her. And now she's...gone. Ruined. She betrayed everyone I care about. I thought I'd learned these things and they didn't matter. I could just—go on. But I can no' do it. Tis as though I've lost her all over again, only this time is worse, because there's nothin' left to love."

With a groan of remorse, Robert drew her down and cradled her. "I'm sorra, my lassie, my Caelia, my love. When I came here...of all the things I considered...I never thought of that. Of yer grief and yer loss. I ne'er thought of the hurt twould cause ye. I'm so sorra, so verra sorra. Can ye forgive me?"

Silence lay upon them, still and heavy, until she answered, "Tis no' yer fault she was...what she was. I would've come to know it sometime, when I learned the truth. At least now ye're here to hold me. Doesn't mean the pain will go right away, but someday. Tis all I ask."

Caelia wanted to forget just now, so she kissed him as she ran her fingertips up his arm to his shoulder. She frowned when she felt a ridged indentation. A scar—a very deep one. How had she missed it when she explored his body earlier? "What's this, Robert Hamilton?"

Before he could answer, she continued the path up his shoulder to his neck, where she found another scar that began just below his ear. As she pushed his hair aside, two voices sounded in her memory. *I did hear once, about Red Rory, that in a close call with a British officer, he was cut with a heated sabre on his shoulder*, Robert had said as they left the fairy cave behind. *I heard it too, but twas his ear, and the mark turned the hair it touched to a streak of white, tellin' everyone who came close enough that he was a hero.* It was getting dark, but in the fading light of day and the new light of the moon, she could just see a small streak of white directly above the scar on his ear. It was too small to show through the thick hair on top, but there was no question about its existence.

She sat back as if the air had been punched out of her. "Red Rory!" she gasped.

He was beside her in an instant. "Please listen to me, Caelia—"

"*Ye* were the boy hero everyone talked about? *Ye?*"

"Aye, weel, tis no as astonishin' as all that, surely." He was affronted, hoping she would not recognize what it meant.

"I'll wager yer hair was never that color red," she accused him, smiling crookedly.

"No. Twas a wig, to make certain Cumberland's soldiers remembered only that. They believed all us savages looked alike anyway."

Then it struck her and the blood drained from her face. "Twas ye then...ye were here when I was a bairn. That's how ye knew how to find the cave, is't no'?"

He had been afraid of this. A new lie for her to grasp and hold against him. He should have remembered the cursed scars.

"Is't no'?" she repeated.

"Aye, but Caelia—"

Only the blessed can find the fairy cave; tis no' for the likes of ordinary mortals. Red Rory was blessed; every Highlander would agree. She was in shock, but only for a moment. Because if anything proved his loyalty to the Jacobites, to the Highlanders, this did. "So I'm guessin' yer name is no' Robert Hamilton?"

He watched her warily for a sign of anger or rejection, but for once could not tell what she was thinking. He decided to behave as if nothing were wrong. "Rory MacGregor, at yer service. Which is why—"

Throwing her arms around him, she kissed him on the lips. "A bonnier name by far than the other. Tis pleased to meet ye, I am, Rory MacGregor."

"Which is why," he continued as if she had not interrupted, though he held her close and did not intend to let her go, "I was never in the British army. Robert Hamilton was, but Robert Hamilton never existed."

Chapter 21

Alarmed, Caelia held his cheeks in the butterfly cup of her hands. "But they'll call ye a deserter and come searchin' for ye." She stared into the calmness of his eyes, trying to make him absorb her urgency. "But we've a tunnel and places we can hide ye on the Hill. No matter how long it takes."

"Ye're no frightened of the soldiers?" he asked.

She shook her head firmly. "Nay. If they threaten my home or those I love, I'll fight them with a pitchfork if I must."

Her lips were set in a strong, thin line, and she curled her hands into tight fists, breathing heavily with the fierceness of her passion. Rory, who had just minutes past been Robert, believed every word she said. "Ye're a wonder, *mo-cridhe*, my heart. But ye need no' be afraid. The British'll no' be comin' after me. I signed a document before I left, resigning my commission."

She sat back, regarding him pensively. "Why?"

"I'm no' certain, except—" he broke off, rubbing his chin while he considered his answer. "I'd begun to forget who I really was, I suppose. I knew deep down, but here and here," he touched his heart and his head, "the lines between Rory MacGregor and Robert Hamilton began to blur. That terrified me more than a musket ball or a bayonet, more even than a claymore."

"I understand," Caelia murmured, "all too well. But then why did ye come here to blur the lines around my mother? To obliterate them? Why, Rory? Because ye were unhappy as yerself?"

His eyes felt damp with tears at the sound of his true name: the name he had not heard for many years. It had once been a source of pride to his mother and his clan, but then he had disappeared to join the army. He doubted if they knew that for sure, but was certain they suspected. They would not welcome him home and call him Rory again. But Caelia had, the young, inexperienced woman who was not afraid of the whole British army. The place where the name had pierced him ached with both joy and apprehension.

He shook his head to clear it. *Caelia asked me a question. What was it? Ah, why did I come here to Fairies' Haven.* "Because I promised myself I would one day. Twas my last duty as a soldier, to set things right here."

"But are they?" Her voice was barely above a whisper.

"Are they what?"

"Right. Have ye set things right?"

He could tell by the question in her golden-brown eyes that she was hurting. "Ye know they aren't. No' yet. Even if I could leave ye, which I never will again, I would no' do it now, like this."

She did not respond at once, and the hint of a breeze rustled the pine needles and the new leaves of hawthorn, beech and oak. She caught the slightest scent of water lapping, splashing over stones, and the tension in her body dissolved. She nodded, rose and offered her hand. "Come," she said, "There're things I want to show ye."

~ * ~

Stealthily, Caelia led him up the stairs circling the tower at the end of the huge house where her room was.

Rory held back. "Are ye sure?" he asked for the third time. "What if they find us?"

"Ye're only here to look, Rory MacGregor, and no' at me. If they find us, weel, mayhap tis time for them to begin gettin' to know ye."

He was appalled by her casual attitude until he realized what he had not noticed in the fading light of gloaming.

There was a smile in her voice. Though he knew he should refuse to go farther, he trusted her and returned her smile.

"Hush ye now," she warned as she turned the key and swung open the iron door to the inside. "I know Papa and Clare are weel and deeply asleep, for they must be up before dawn, but we don't want to be takin' a risk."

By the time they reached her rooms, both were out of breath. Caelia closed the door quietly. Clare had left one oil lamp burning low, as she always did. Caelia turned it up and added another, then motioned for him to remove his coat. She put her plaid on top of it and they spread both on the floor to sit on.

Rory looked at the portraits and landscapes propped against the walls. Even in the flickering lamplight he could see how talented she was. The landscapes, all of places he had seen around the glen since he'd been here, practically leapt off the page with the intensity of vivid color and life and...he tried to think of the word, and then it came to him: depth. The portraits had that same quality. He felt he could reach out and touch the faces, as if they would be round and whole, rather than flat and lifeless. "They're incredible, Caelia! How do ye do it? They're so real and yet fanciful at the same time."

"Tis mostly the pastels that give them the immediacy, the life. Ye can be spontaneous, ye ken, without havin' to wait for the paint to dry or to make allowances for the change in color. I studied Rosalba Carreira, the first well-known pastelist. She worked in Paris as many of them do— or at least they study there. Jean Baptiste Simeon and Jean Etienne Liotard have followed her, and now Maurice de la Tour. They do wondrous things I can only marvel at." She paused, cheeks pink with delight. "I'll never be like them, nor do I wish to be. All I know is when the color is in my hands, my fingers and eyes take over and I'm in another, mystical place."

She was radiant as she spoke of her art. Rory was

enchanted. "Ye're aye a most beautiful woman, Caelia Rose."

"I always thought I was rather ordinary. No' really lovely. No' like my mother..." she trailed off and the effervescence drained away. "Tis what I wanted to show ye." Opening Lila's chest, she took out a sketch, one canvas and one piece of vellum with her attempts at her mother's portraits, then the small stack of self-portraits, including the canvas she'd painted the day Robert Hamilton had appeared in Glen Affric. Only now he was Rory MacGregor and he was sitting in her bedroom.

Without a word, she spread them out in the lamplight. He looked at the three first. "These are of yer mother."

It was not a question and she did not reply.

"Did ye do them in the last few days? There's a great deal of anger here."

"No, before," she said. "I was tryin' to make her beautiful, exquisite, as I believed she was. These—" she pointed to the snakes; the deep shadow; and in the third one, Lila Rose with a malicious grin on her face, beckoning toward churning water like a siren toward the rocks—"were no' intentional. There've been many others, but twas always the same."

Rory regarded the portraits in silence. "Ye could no' make her into what she was not. Some part of ye must've known—"

Caelia bowed her head. "No, twas the Sight. I told ye, it comes out in my paintin's and sketches. Twas a message I refused to see." To divert him from further discussion on the subject, she indicated the images of herself. "Tis the same with me."

Sifting through the sketches, Rory was shocked to realize they were meant to be of Caelia. Some had her hair, or the shape of her eyes, but the color was never quite right. More often than not, the face was amorphous, undefined, as if she could not trace her own cheekbones and jawline. The one she had done the day he arrived was quite lovely—a mermaid out of water without her tail—but it did not look like his Caelia: except, once more, for the hair.

"Why do ye think tis, Rory?" She was tense, awaiting his reply. "I feel like I've been wanderin', weak and daft like a bairn. Knowin' nothin' about anythin', waitin' for others to tell me who I am."

He turned to face her, taking her hands and squeezing them tight. "That's no' true. Ye're strong, Caelia, stronger and more certain than ye know. Ye have faith and integrity and honesty and loyalty."

She shook her head. "Those arena strengths. Tis easy to be those things."

Rory was stunned. "If ye knew how many people are traitors and villains because they're weak, because they're untrustworthy, so they can't trust another, evil because tis easier to be greedy than good. Ye have power in your soul, Caelia."

"I don't want to have power," she cried. "SHE had power, and twas unkind. Ugly. I never wanted to be like her." She gaped, not believing what she had just said.

But he believed it. "What do ye mean?" he asked gently.

"I see it when my aunt and my father speak of her, even now. They say only good things, and smile with warm voices, but I see doubt. I see how they fear what I might think. I see resentment sometimes, and sometimes anger, bitterness and grief beyond bearin'. I ken my mother created those feelin's, because they only come when Aunt Clare and Papa speak of *her*. They think I'm blind and only hear what they tell me, but I see. I see too much."

He recognized in that moment that he had given her too little credit. At first she had appeared to be content, trusting everyone, but she'd had to fight for that happiness. And that too took a strength he had not imagined. Yet he had admired her from the first time they met, from the moment she threatened to get the musket if he did not go. Now, finally he understood why. "Ye've drawn them as well, haven't ye?"

"Aye, though I was forbidden to. The only thing they ever forbad. But I could no' obey them. I could see they were hurtin' and I wanted to know the truth." She gathered her hair together and ran her hands up and down the abundant swathe. "But after I drew them, I could no' help them. I saw and felt the worry they had built into walls, keepin' them apart from one another, but I could no' begin to tear the walls down."

The lamplight wavered and sputtered, casting her face now in shadow, now in light. "Papa and Clare gave me such a happy childhood. Only now do I realize how difficult that was for them."

He took her in his arms and kissed her in reassurance.

"All I wanted was to make the hurtin' stop. Sometimes twas just too hard, and I escaped into my paintin'. Twas selfish of me, was't no'?"

He kissed her eyelids, her nose, her lips ever so lightly. "Twas wise, my love. Twould have done them no good for ye to suffer with them. Twould have broken them if they'd known. Do ye even realize how big a heart ye have? Can ye understand yer own courage and compassion? Ye're amazin', my Caelia. There's no other like ye."

Chapter 22

She awakened smiling, then sat up frantically, but there was no sign of Rory. She had fallen asleep in his arms last night, and he'd apparently removed her clothes and put her to bed in her chemise. Her long hair was hanging in a rough braid with ends sticking out everywhere. *So that's something he's no' trained in,* she thought with a grin.

She rose, wide awake and eager to meet the day. After a breakfast of cold mutton, milk, cheese, and apples, which she enjoyed with Clare and Malcolm, steering the conversation to everyday things and far away from the subject of Lila Rose. She offered to cancel her appointment with Graham Gordon the carpenter, who was carving novel tools for her to use to create new textures in her pastels, but her aunt and father bid her be on her way. They too wanted to pretend it was a day like any other.

~ * ~

Caelia had told Rory where she was going, so he waited until she left before approaching the Hill of the Hounds. He simply could not bring himself to think of it as Fairies' Haven. He assured himself—again—that he did not believe in magic, no matter what he had seen in the last few days.

On that thought, he reached the huge front door and let the ornate silver knocker fall three times. He tried to look confident, but he was apprehensive. *I've the right of it*, he told himself silently, but that made no difference. A young woman he guessed was the chamber maid—Caelia had told him they had only one—opened the door.

"I'm here to see Malcolm Rose and Clare MacKinley. Ye can tell them Robert Hamilton is callin'."

The maid disappeared and returned immediately to lead him to a dark room lined floor-to-ceiling with bookshelves and dominated by a huge old mahogany desk. So they'd chosen what must be Rose's office instead of the sitting room or morning room. This was not going to be easy. But he'd known that all along.

They left him waiting for quite a while. He had expected that. He spent the time perusing Rose's manuscripts, books, and piles of broadsheets. He was surprised at how many works of music there were: songbooks and folios and sheet music for harpsichord and cello. Rory was intrigued.

When they finally arrived, they greeted him in as few words as minimal politeness allowed, then Malcolm sat on the far side of the desk and Clare on the arm of the heavy desk chair. They stared at him with eyebrows raised, exactly as if they had rehearsed it. He noticed Rose barely touched the woman's elbow, but she sat up straighter, looking more confident.

"Weel then, what is't ye want?" Clare asked at last.

He decided to get straight to the point. "I want ye to tell Caelia the rest. All of it."

Clare stood abruptly. "All of what? Who are ye to tell us—? Ye dinna ken what ye're talkin' about."

"But I do, Mistress MacKinley. I know exactly. I was there that day, ye see."

"What day? Dinna be ridiculous! Ye would've been but a bairn."

Malcolm was standing beside her now, hands on her shoulders protectively. "Ye'd better go," he said in the rumbling voice of the laird of the manor.

"I must answer the lady. I'll no' be rude. The day yer sister died, Mistress. Aye, I was a bairn of nine, my father but a few days dead at the Battle of Culloden Moor. My name, then and now, is Rory MacGregor."

Her face went pale and her grey eyes wide. "It canna

be."

"But tis," he insisted.

"I always knew ye'd make us pay," she replied indignantly.

Malcolm turned her to face him. "What's the lad goin' on about? Who is he?"

Sighing raggedly, she tried to free herself from her brother-in-law's grasp. "His mam and he helped us get away from that awful place. I told ye about them. She'd just lost a bairn and she fed Caelia and brewed broths to make her strong enough to travel. Rory," she waved her hand in his general direction, "went out and caught dinner every day, and watched for soldiers and kept us safe. I tried to give them silver when I'd recovered from my shock and Caelia was well enough for us to come home, but they'd take no' a farthin'. I wondered since if we'd no' have to pay some other way."

"I'm no' here for that. We were happy to help, grateful to have somethin' to think of besides the lost bairn and my father. Grateful we could at least salvage somethin' from that tragedy. I *still* want nothin' except ye tell Caelia the whole truth." He looked Malcolm in the eye. "Ye have to trust her. She's strong enough and wise enough to understand. If ye keep her in the dark as ye've been doin', part of her'll never grow up, never become a full woman. She's so much already: a seer, a healer, a friend, a confidant, an impressive artist, a singer. Do you know how much strength it takes to be all those things to many people? Trust her enough to tell her the truth, or I will."

"Tis no' your responsibility or your right," Malcolm said gruffly.

"Exactly."

"She's happy now. Leave her alone." The threat in Clare's tone was clear as the daylight.

"Is she? Or is she merely content? There's a difference, ye ken." He gazed at Clare. "Or do ye?"

She glanced down for only a moment, but it was enough.

"Ye do know. How can ye let her exist with no family of her own, no love of her own, no passion?"

"Are you offerin' yerself for the job? I can see ye've bewitched her. Is that why ye came? To tell her the truth and make her hate us? Or to make her love ye?" Rose's face turned red as he fed his own anger. "Ye're a spy, a British soldier. She told us. What do you really want from us? Why have ye come?"

"My commandin' officer, General Kingston sent me."

Profound silence fell over the dark room. "That butcher—that bastard…" Clare sputtered.

Rose stood rigid. ""Why would he do that?" The words came out stridently.

"I think ye know why." Rory had the good grace to study his shoes with apparent interest.

"All I know is ye're no' welcome here. Get out before she hears ye. Get out before tis too late. Get out, get out, get out!" Clare's voice rose on every word. She did not care if she was making sense. She just wanted this man who knew too much to go.

Rory stood rooted to the spot on the blue and gray carpet.

"What will we have if ye take her from us? If ye make her hate us? What will we have if she finds out the truth?" She wept, clasping her hands together so tightly that she cried out at the pain.

Slowly, tenderly, Malcolm Rose put his hand on her shoulder. He didn't realize until that moment how very dear she was to him. "Clare, *mo-cridhe*, ye know our Caelia better than that. I'm thinkin' she'd never turn her back on her family." He forgot about Rory as his heart pounded so hard he thought it might burst. "Besides, we'll always have each other. Finally and for good—each other."

At his gentle touch, she turned to look at him,

bemused. "Surely ye don't mean…" In spite of herself, she could not quite hide the glimmer of hope in her eyes.

"I do, *mo-charaid*. I knew it when I was young, every day we grew together side by side. But Lila made me forget. She did that to a lot of men. It took me a long time to remember, but no' nearly as long as it did to find the courage to admit it to ye. I love ye. Only ye. The shadow of that other woman haunts my daughter's dreams, not mine."

Her eyes brimmed with tears but she fought them back. She would not weep in front of this stranger. Except she saw by his kind expression he had known of Malcolm's feelings all along. Could he be right about Caelia as well?

"I'm no' actually a British soldier, Miss MacKinley. Tis true I work for General Kingston as his valet and right-hand man. I've no' always held that position, but I've worked for him—or pretended to—since I was 10-years-old. I convinced him he needed me as he needed no one else, until he trusted me as he trusted no one else. But seein' as my name is no' and never was Robert Hamilton, I can hardly be called a true British officer."

"Ye mean ye've been spyin' on him all this time?"

"Just watchin' to make sure he and his men did as little harm as possible. Though he lost his bravado when Lila Rose died. She broke him and he's never been the same."

"Neither have I," Malcolm Rose said. "It took me a long time to understand I'm a better man because of that."

"Then can ye no' tell Caelia?"

Malcolm and Clare exchanged haunted glances. "She'll never forgive us," they said to each other.

"Have a wee bit of faith," Rory MacGregor encouraged them. He'd had none when he first came here, but Caelia had changed that. She had changed everything.

Chapter 23

Caelia knew something was wrong the minute she entered the house. Her portfolio case still in hand she crept forward, weighed down by the unnatural stillness: an expectant stillness, just waiting for something to break it. She did not wish to be the one to do it. Noticing that the morning room door was open, she moved toward it on tiptoe. She had the sense there had been quiet conversation a moment past, but that the sound of the front door closing stopped it abruptly. The damp spring air hung heavy in the stone front hall, and the shadows in the corners seemed deep and menacing. *Ye're imaginin' things, Caelia Rose,* she scolded herself silently.

Determined to conquer her anxiety, she pushed the door fully open. And ceased, frozen, on the threshold.

Rory, Clare and Malcolm rose as one when they saw her.

"What..." Caelia swallowed dryly, "are ye doing here?" Something in their attitude warned her that the stillness had come from within them. All three together in some joint enterprise.

"Caelia, we need to speak with ye."

The tone of her father's voice—kind but resolute—turned his daughter's anxiety to dread.

"Come." Clare stepped forward, opening her arms, but her niece wanted to run.

Forcing herself to remain where she was, Caelia, breathed deeply, steeling herself. She would not let them see her fear. She swore she would be stronger than they imagined she could. She knew something terrible was coming; she could see it in their eyes. Rory would not even look at her.

When she was ready, she crossed the vivid colors of the Brussels carpet and sat in the tapestried wingback chair, her portfolio at her feet. "Aye?" she murmured.

Her father and aunt sat side-by-side on the matching settee, but Rory remained standing. Something had changed between Malcolm and Clare, but Caelia could not decide what. Just now she was blind to all but the waiting stillness.

"I have a story to tell," her aunt said at last, with a sidelong glance at Rory. "Tis no verra happy, but tis one we think ye should know."

Malcolm covered her clenched hand with his and she released some of the tension. Caelia's eyes widened. So that was it. She had only a moment to glance from one to the other, smiling, before Clare began.

"Twas back in 1746 toward the end of the Forty-Five....

~ * ~

Clare MacKinley had been living in the Highland forest for months, delivering messages back and forth to the Jacobite leaders, as she desperately searched for her kidnapped sister in the British camps and forts. Both endeavors were extremely dangerous; she was used to her heart pounding and her blood racing in her ears as she hid beneath dirt and leaves and pine needles when British patrols passed by. She was dressed as a man—the only way she could move easily from place to place—and wore her hair pinned up beneath a brown wig, which she covered with a black tricorn hat.

She had been chased by soldiers six times, by opponents to the Jacobites twice, in a knife fight more than once, and shot at three times. She was grateful the two men with knives had been drunk as well, and that British muskets were hard to aim, though just five minutes past a musket ball had screamed across her shoulder. She was always afraid, and could only imagine the horrors her sister Lila was being subjected to. The more Clare suffered from exposure, threats to her life from the British, and the importance of the messages she carried, the more resolute she became.

The savagery, death and blood she witnessed had increased one-hundredfold in the last few days, since the rumored slaughter at Culloden Moor. She suspected the horrific accounts she was hearing were true from the way the British were spreading the carnage through the woods and hollows where she hid. Another Jacobite fleeing the soldiers had told her that morning that Major-General Jonathan Kingston was camped just south of Culloden.

Clare was almost there and certain, this time, that he and his men would not slip away before she had her chance to find Lila.

Now she stopped, leaning against a sturdy oak for support, to examine the wound. It was bleeding profusely so she used the dirk she carried in her boot to cut off the bottom of her shirt. She had a tiny otter bladder of wine hanging around her neck. This she poured over the wound, biting on a thick twig as she did so. Then she bound it with the torn portion of her shirt.

It was a long time before she could gather the strength to push herself away from the oak and continue on her way. She was exhausted, with blisters on her feet and hands. "But I'm almost there," she whispered, watching and listening for the sound of hoofbeats or footsteps.

She came upon a riderless horse without English colors and decided to take the chance. The saddle was worn, the horse sturdy but nothing to look at; it would not draw attention. Clare rode it the last few miles, and was thankful for it, as the ground became littered everywhere with bodies and mud turned red with blood. She had seen killing aplenty in the past months, but this was too terrible to take in. She wanted to close her eyes, but would not give up guiding the horse as best she could through the remnants of the massacre.

Finally she was in view of Kingston's camp. She knew his personal standard well enough by now. She picked out his tent from the low branch of a hawthorn tree. She could see most of the soldiers were gone, though the battle must have been over for several days. Out hunting down the survivors, were they? She shuddered and crossed the several yards to the camp by weaving back and forth through what sparse cover there was.

She noticed a few men gathered at the center when she reconnoitered from the tree. She hoped they would not be a threat. *I'm comin', Lila. Comin'. Be ready to run!* She knew her sister could not hear, but she was so excited, so full of hope that at last Lila would be free. As would Clare.

As she approached, she saw women in the crowd as well, washerwomen, no doubt, and doxies for the men. They traveled with every army. She looked about, searching for Lila, but her sister was not there. Slipping quietly in among the small crowd, she wondered what they were staring at. And then she saw her.

Lila Rose was standing at the flap door to the commander's tent, apparently pleading, while he— definitely a major-general by his colors—shook his head and pointed toward the crowd. Clare was stunned to realize her sister held a young baby in her arms. She felt more than a little ill, moving surreptitiously forward through the crowd until their voices came to her.

"Please, Jonathan, I love ye. Please don't send me away. I'll do anything ye ask. Anything. I beg ye." Lila's golden eyes were full of desire, her face flushed, her entreaty passionate.

Nausea rose in Clare's throat. For a long moment she could not comprehend what she was seeing. All she knew was she had never seen her sister this sincere before.

Kingston lowered his voice, and from the disgust in his

expression, Clare became fully aware of what was happening. Lila was in love, and the major-general was rejecting her: her and her baby—which must be his. Clare's eyes stung with frozen fury that she could not allow herself to feel. Her sister had stolen Malcolm away, and yet she never loved him. She loved this man—this British traitor to all they believed in.

Suddenly there was a scuffle, and Lila backed away, Kingston's pistol in one hand, the baby in the other. "I dinna give my heart for free, ye ken. But ye've taken it from me and now ye'd send me away? How can I bear it? How can I live without ye?" Her face was ugly and swollen with tears, her fine blonde hair a tangled mess. "I'll kill ye. Ye and yer child!"

Clare's mouth fell open in horror.

Some of the men pointed their rifles with attached bayonets, but Kingston waved them off. "You would have to reload the pistol. You wouldn't know how." He sounded calm and unconcerned.

Lila's mouth curved in a clever smile. "Do ye think I've no' watched ye as ye load and fire? Do ye think I'm fool enough to leave myself unarmed? I've practiced when ye're out talkin' and drinkin' with the men. I've used yer spare when I couldna get this one." She cocked the hammer one-handed with astonishing ease. "If tis the baby ye dinna want, I'll rid ye of her, Jonny. Jest tell me what to do."

Clare could not move or make a sound; she was paralyzed by this woman she'd thought she knew so well.

"I told you to go. I will not be the cuckold your husband is. Go." His voice trembled slightly, but apparently Lila did not hear.

She raised the pistol again, and just when the men began to charge forward, turned it to her ear and pulled the trigger.

Chapter 24

Caelia could not breathe. Her stays were too tight. Or was it the way Clare sank into Malcolm, exhausted and drained? Or perhaps, just perhaps, it was the story of her aunt's suffering and her mother's death. Malcolm Rose had told her Clare was in danger back then, but she had not really understood until now. And though she had learned many things about Lila Rose, she had never expected this—this revulsion. And following all too quickly, pity. She had wanted to know who her mother was. Well now she did. And she could not hear or breathe or think.

"You're tired," Malcolm said, gathering Clare into his arms to let her absorb his strength. "Let Rory finish."

"What?" Caelia's head snapped up. "Rory? What does he know of it?"

Her parents turned to him in silent entreaty.

With compassion and apology in his hazel eyes, he sat on the footstool belonging to her chair. "I can tell the rest—"

"There's more?" She choked out the words.

"What happened to ye and Mistress MacKinley afterward."

"And ye know this because…."

"I was there," he told her softly. "I was nine-years-old at the time."

Caelia shook her head back and forth, back and forth. "No!" She tried to stand, but her legs would not hold her. She fell back into the chair, curling her feet beneath her green skirt with the pockets, moving her knees as far back as possible so Rory would not touch them accidentally. *Ye were there,* she thought, *at my mother's humiliation, at my mother's death, and ye said nothing?* It was one thing that her parents had not told her; she suspected she would understand why when she got over her shock. But Rory? Again?

She was chilled to the bone and her stays pressed tight against her frigid skin. "Why did ye come here?"

"I told ye before, to make things right." He reached for her but she shrank away.

"I dinna believe ye. But tell yer story and then be gone. For good this time. Forever, do ye ken?" She imagined her words hitting the warm air of the morning room in cloudy bursts, like warm breath in winter. Only now the process was reversed. Her breath was cold, cold, cold, and the room was temperate from the fire and the momentary sun outside the window.

"Caelia, please!"

She could see deep sorrow in Rory's face, but she did not care. "Tell me."

Unwillingly, he began. "The two of us—Clare and I—both got to ye at the same time. Ye were still lyin' in the crook of yer mother's arm, and we whisked ye away before anyone noticed in the confusion. The last thing I saw was the Major-General kneelin' o'er yer mother's body.

"I took ye and yer aunt to a cave hidden deep in the mountains where even the determined British could no' find it. My own mother was hidin' there. My da' was killed at Culloden, ye see, and the Butcher was seekin' all MacGregors still livin'. My mam saw at once that Clare's wound needed tendin' and ye were weak and undernourished. Yer aunt told the story of her months searchin' and what she'd found, and my mam took ye in. We cared for ye till ye were both healthy enough to travel, and Cumberland's lust for blood had abated."

"They saved our lives, Caelia. We'd no' be here now, neither ye or me, without them."

The girl nodded mutely. She was incapable of any other action.

"Meanwhile, I went back each day, for I'd wheedled my way into bein' Kingston's boot boy, and sometimes I cleaned his weapons. I wanted to be close to the British plans, at first to save my father, and then to avenge him. After yer mother was dead, all his affection returned. He had her buried formally with what flowers he could find, and later he went back to raise the tombstone he'd had carved for her. With her blood still on his hands that day, he started askin' for his daughter, though I could see he'd not know what to do with ye if he had ye. So we kept ye hidden."

Turning to Malcolm Rose, Caelia said, "That...man thought he was my father. Is't true?" She held her breath as she waited, counting the seconds, the years, the eternity that had passed since the day her mother died.

Rose stood, straightening to his full six foot. "Tis true my wife was with him all those months, but—"

Clare stood beside him and took his hand. "But she also came home for a time. Remember I told ye that, Caelia? Before Kingston took her again. Twould have been about the time of conception."

"So what're ye sayin'?" The girl clenched her teeth to keep them from chattering.

Rory looked from Rose to his daughter and back again. For the first time, he was the one with questions in his eyes.

"That we can no' say for certain who yer father is," Malcolm said as gently as he could. He gazed at her mournfully, but his face, tanned from the sun and lined from years of doubt and pain—was full of love. "I'd give anythin' I have to tell ye tis me, but I've sworn to speak only the truth from now on. Still, it doesn't change how I feel about ye. I never cared whether twas his blood or mine that flowed in yer veins. Ye're *my* daughter, and always will be."

"And mine," Clare added, slipping her arm through Malcolm's. "From the moment I first saw yer tiny face."

Caelia was lost. Without moving, she was searching blindly through a fog so thick she could not see her own hands. Somewhere in the distant back of her mind, she knew they were telling the truth, but it did not lift the thick cocoon around her or show her the way out. She was going to cry, and they were all watching. She had to get away from those piercing eyes filled with pity.

Instinctively she ran. Out of the house, down the hill and into the forest. The cool, welcoming forest, where the leaves of the hawthorn and beeches and oak would conceal her anguish. The light poured through the canopy overhead in streams, piercing the fog around her, making the forest a sacred place, a place of magic. She found a hummock where she knelt, her red plaid over her head and shoulders, in the secret cathedral where she hoped find the healing power that would save her soul.

Chapter 25

Rory found her there, asleep in the ferns, her face streaked with tears. She must have had a dark pastel and piece of parchment in her pocket, for she had sketched two faces on the fragment: Lila Rose and Jonathan Kingston. He stared at the latter for some time. He was certain she had never seen the man, yet the likeness was startling.

Rory sat on a large tilted rock for a moment to catch his breath. He would wake her in a moment, but for now, he wanted just to look at her, peaceful in sleep in spite of the tear tracks on her cheeks. *What will ye say to me when ye awake?* he wondered. *Will ye ever forgive me for knowin' too much?* His heart ached at the answer he feared. And he would not really blame her. But he could not live without her. He had seen what a life without love could do to a man.

"Rory?"

"Aye, lass, I'm here." The sound of her voice was so sweet. He wanted to hold her until the pain went, but he did not dare touch her.

Caelia rubbed a finger across each eye as she sat up, frowning.

Rory thought it the most graceful gesture he had ever seen.

Glancing about in some surprise, she tried to remember how she came to be sleeping in the forest. Then it all came back to her. She gasped once at the shock, then saw the fog had lifted. She was no longer lost, but knew exactly where she was. How that had come about she did not know, but she could not help feeling the fairies and their enchantments had been involved. She faintly remembered the brush of tiny whispers against her cheeks, the puff of

126

sweet breath—one upon another, upon another—and the music of hundreds of wings in flight, singing her to rest and compassion and peace. She smiled softly to herself. The fairies had returned. "What is't ye hold in yer hand?" she asked Rory.

Wordlessly, he handed her the bit of parchment. She examined it as if she'd never seen it before. "They both seem very sad, very lonely. The major-general's no' frightenin' at all. He's just an old man."

"A general now, though tis meaningless to him. He's old and sorely alone, but that was his choice."

"He...he sent ye, did he no'?"

There was no anger in her question, but that did not reassure him. He feared her indifference more than her rage. "He asked if I would seek ye out a while past, and I did, though for reasons of my own. He wanted me to ask if ye would go to him, though I warned him twas unlikely."

She nodded thoughtfully, her heart beating dully. "And what were *yer* reasons?"

Rory met her golden-brown eyes. "That day, and those that followed, were forever burned into my memory. I could no' forget yer helplessness or Clare MacKinley's courage. Tis why, when the major-general received orders to destroy this place, I came as Red Rory to warn ye, though I knew he'd never do it. For Lila's sake. I just wanted to be sure ye were as safe, as ye were in our secret cave." He paused to take a deep breath.

Caelia listened with shimmering eyes, holding onto her sketches, trying with all her heart and soul to believe him.

"I'd been wantin' to come again, to see how ye'd grown and if ye were happy. But I was a bitter man myself, havin' lost so much in the Forty-Five. And workin' for a man who'd lost everythin' as weel. When I saw how young and free and happy ye were, I feared ye might be more like yer mother than yer aunt. Tis why I pushed ye so. But I was wrong. So verra wrong, *mo-cridhe*. I hope ye can forgive me."

She stared at her hands, then forced herself to meet his gaze. "Whatever I am, I am because my father and Clare raised me, nourished me, loved me, spoiled me. They were there when I needed comfort or when I wanted to share a small triumph. They accepted the crofters and their children as my friends, though most who lived in manor houses would have shunned such society. My parents cared because I cared. I know not all families are like that. I'm gey lucky in those I love. All of them." She reached across to take his hand.

"Are ye sure?" he asked. "I know I've hurt ye and confused ye."

"I was only confused because I met one Rory—or Robert—at a time. I had to come to accept each one, just as I accepted each bit of the truth I learned about my mother. Mayhap, while ye've been here, ye've discovered things about yerself ye never knew. I've learned many things about me as I learned to know the woman who bore me and my parents who tried to protect me."

Rory's eyes filmed with moisture. "Aye, we're both different now, and mayhap ready for each other." He leaned forward and she met him halfway, cupping his cheek in her hand and meeting his cool lips with hers. Soon both were more than warm, but he stopped the kiss and drew her onto his lap.

"Do ye realize, lass, that ye've sketched yer mother without evil darkenin' her face?"

She looked down at the portrait of Lila with one tear on her cheek. "Aye. Tis from the Sight. See how sad she is in every line? Both she and her lover."

"What about the tear?" Rory asked. "Is that from grief over losin' Kingston?"

Caelia shook her head and thought for a moment. "No. Over losin' my father and Clare and me. Over all the memories she never had. Tis only one tear, because I don't think she realized how great that loss was."

"But ye do?"

"Aye," she murmured, "I finally do." Her smile was soft and poignant and his throat tightened at the lone tear on her own cheek.

"Thank ye," she said, "for helpin' me see."

"No, Caelia, twas ye who opened my eyes. And do ye ken what I realized when I saw yer paintin's the other night, and now with these sketches? The magic never left this place. It's been here all along—in ye. In what ye see and feel and sketch and who ye are."

He noticed there was something on the back of the parchment and turned it over to see a skillful portrait of Caelia. When he looked up, she was smiling.

"Tis strange that no' until I felt my heart had been torn from me did I realize twas no' true. Twas there all along, just as ye said, whole and strong and true. And the people I love are here with me, and no' lost on some distant moor. I was growin' and becomin' who I am every minute of every day since I was born. I've always known who that is, I simply didna look inside and see." Her smile grew brighter and wider as she spoke. "I'm Caelia Rose, myself. Just that."

"Aye," Rory murmured, "and tis more than enough."

About Kathryn Lynn Davis

Kathryn Lynn Davis was born with what the ancient Celts called "the fatal gift of the imagination: a crown of stars and a stinging sword." She had no choice but to become a writer. Since Scotland is the home of her heart, and she loves history (having a Masters in the subject), it was inevitable that she should write historical novels, most of which are set in Scotland. An award winning, New York Times best-seller, she has published eight historical novels and one historical novella.

Kathryn has a BA in English and history from the University of California, Riverside, where she graduated Magna Cum Laude, Phi Beta Kappa. She also received her MA in history there.

Toward the end of the 20th century, she gave up writing out of frustration. Only when she discovered Indie publishing did she return to her love of writing with great enthusiasm. She has re-published part of her backlist as e-books: *Child of Awe*, and the Too Deep For Tears Trilogy: *Too Deep for Tears, All We Hold Dear,* and *Somewhere Lies the Moon*.

A Tear for Memory along with a second novella, *Highland Awakening*, are prequels to her Too Deep Trilogy. They are both available as a single e-books and paperbacks.

Recently she reworked and published *Sing To Me Of Dreams* the sequel for which, *Weave for Me a Dream*, will be released Fall 2016. She's so excited by all this activity, and all the new friends--both authors and readers--that she's made on Facebook.

Follow Kathryn Davis on Facebook:
https://www.facebook.com/kathrynlynndavis.

Other Titles From Duncurra

Highland Awakening

Can the transforming power of magic help two people on a perilous journey create a miracle—even when one of them doesn't believe?

Since she lost her brother and nearly her father, Esmé Rose fears the world beyond her family and her garden. But one year when winter clings overlong, a dream begins to haunt her, forcing her to take a journey and face a challenge more difficult than she could ever imagine.

Magnus MacLeod is a skilled healer, always curious to know more. He, too, is called by a dream he doesn't quite believe in, despite its physical effects on him. He and Esmé travel a treacherous road that takes them to a magical place. There they must put aside their feelings for one another— and their difference in beliefs—long enough to make a miracle.

Sing to Me of Dreams

One woman's journey of discovery...through all the mysteries of the human heart.

As a child, Saylah held the magic and wisdom of her Salish Indian people. But when tragedy ravages the Salish, she must leave them for the world of the Ivys – an English/Scottish family whose traditions are as strange to her as her spirit world is to them. The Ivys have come to fertile British Columbia in search of paradise, but the secrets and mysteries surrounding them are overwhelming – until Saylah comes to help them understand the darkness holding them back.

Frustrated Julian Ivy, in whom sophistication and fury entwine, is drawn to Saylah's healing strength and disquieting beauty. Through sorrow and elation, the two discover the fullness of love...but no one can resolve for her the contradictions of her birthright. Following the songs of her heritage, she will finally make the most wrenching choice of all...

Award Winning, Bestselling Author, Lily Baldwin

Jack: A Scottish Outlaw

Freedom is not won...it is stolen

Jack MacVie and his brother are thieves, robbing English nobles on the road north into Scotland. They're about to attack the Redesdale carriage when another band of villains, after more than Lady Redesdale's coin, sweeps down and steals their prize. Despite his hatred for the English, Jack's conscience forces him to kidnap the lady to save her life.

In the aftermath of the Berwick massacre, Lady Isabella Redesdale's world is shattered. Her mother is dead, her father lost to grief, and she's risking it all, journeying north into war-torn Scotland to be with her sister.

Although they come from different worlds, Jack and Isabella are more alike than they first realize. They both crave freedom from war and despair, but in a world where kings reign and birth dictates one's station, freedom is not won, it is stolen.

Quinn: A Scottish Outlaw

He is an outlaw...And the only man she can trust.

Quinn MacVie is in pursuit of a prize, but it is unlike any plunder he has stolen before. He seeks neither gold nor jewels, but something infinitely more valuable—Lady Catarina Ravensworth. Sent by the lady's sister, who fears Catarina is in danger, Quinn's mission is to steal the lady away from Ravensworth castle. But nothing there is as Quinn expected.

Lady Catarina has been accused of a horrific crime and is forced to run or face a fate worse than death.

But she is not alone.

Thief and Scottish rebel, Quinn MacVie, is at her side. With a price on her head, they must disappear into the wilds of the Scottish Highlands where the only thing greater than the danger following at their heels is the desire burning in their hearts.

Stephanie Joyce Cole

Compass North

Can you ever run away from your own life?

Reeling from the shock of a suddenly shattered marriage, Meredith flees as far from her home in Florida as she can get without a passport: to Alaska.

After a freak accident leaves her presumed dead, she stumbles into a new identity and a new life in a quirky small town. Her friendship with a fiery and temperamental artist and her growing worry for her elderly, cranky landlady pull at the fabric of her carefully guarded secret. When a romance with a local fisherman unexpectedly blossoms, Meredith struggles to find a way to meld her past and present so that she can move into the future she craves.

But someone is looking for her, someone who will threaten Meredith's dream of a reinvented life.

Award Winning, Bestselling Author, Ceci Giltenan

Time Travel Romance:

The Pocket Watch: The Pocket Watch Chronicles

When Maggie Mitchell, is transported to the thirteenth century Highlands will Laird Logan Carr help mend her broken heart or put it in more danger than before?

Generous, kind, and loving, Maggie nearly always puts the needs of others first. So when a mysterious elderly woman gives her an extraordinary pocket watch, telling her it's a conduit to the past, Maggie agrees to give the watch a try, if only to disprove the woman's delusion.
But it works.
Maggie finds herself in the thirteenth century Scottish Highlands, with a handsome warrior who clearly despises her. Her tender soul is caught between her own desire and the disaster she could cause for others. Will she find a way to resolve the trouble and return home within the allotted sixty days? Or will someone worthy earn her heart forever?

The Pocket Watch is available as an e-book, audiobook and paperback.

Once Found: The Pocket Watch Chronicles

Elsie thought she had found love.

The handsome young minstrel awoke her desire and his music fed her soul. But just as love was blossoming, the inconceivable happened—Elsie awoke more than seven hundred years in the future, in the body of Dr. Elizabeth Quinn.

Gabriel Soldani thought he had found love several times, only to have it slip from his grasp. In medical school he had fallen hard for Elizabeth Quinn but their careers led them in different directions. When their paths cross again, he hopes they've been given another chance.

There's only one problem…the woman he's never forgotten doesn't remember him.

Once love is found…and then lost…can it be found again?

The Midwife: The Pocket Watch Chronicles

Can a twenty-first century independent woman find her true destiny, in thirteenth century Scotland?

At his father's bidding, Cade MacKenzie begs a favor from Laird Macrae—Lady MacKenzie desperately needs the renowned Macrae midwife. Laird Macrae has no intention of sending his clan's best, instead he passes off Elsie, a young woman with little experience, as the midwife they seek.

But fate—in the form of a mysterious older woman and an extraordinary pocket watch—steps in.

Elizabeth Quinn, a disillusioned obstetrician, is transported to the thirteenth century. She switched souls with Elsie as the old woman said she would but other things don't go quite as expected. Perhaps most unexpected was falling in love.

Scottish Historical Romance

Highland Revenge

Does he hate her clan enough to visit his vengeance on her? Or will he listen to her secret and his own heart's yearning?

Hatred lives and breathes between medieval clans who often don't remember why feuds began in the shadowed past.

But Eoin MacKay remembers.

He will never forget how he was treated by Bhaltair MacNicol—the acting head of Clan MacNicol. He was lucky to escape alive, and vows to have revenge.

Years later, as laird of Clan MacKay, he gets his chance when he captures Lady Fiona MacNicol. His desire for revenge is strong but he is beguiled by his captive.

Can he forget his stubborn hatred long enough to listen to the secret she has kept for so long? And once he knows the truth, can he show her she is not alone and forsaken? In the end, is he strong enough to fight the combined hostilities and age-old grudges that demand he give her up?

Highland Echoes

Love echoes.

Grace Breive is strong and independent because she has to be. She has a wee daughter to care for and, having lost her parents and husband, has no one else on whom she can rely. Driven from the only home she has ever known, she travels to Castle Sutherland to find a grandmother she never knew she had.

As Laird Sutherland's heir, Bram Sutherland understands his obligation to enter into a political marriage for the good of the clan, but he is captivated by the beautiful and resilient young mother.

Will Bram and Grace follow the dictates of their hearts, or will echoes from the past force them apart?

Highland Angels

Anna MacKay fears the MacLeods. Andrew MacLeod fears love.

Anna, angry with her brother, took a walk to cool her temper. She had no intention of venturing so close to MacLeod territory—until she saw a wee lad fall through the ice.

Andrew becomes enraged when it appears the MacKay lass has abducted his son, his last precious connection to the wife he lost—until he learns the truth. Anna, risked her life to save his beloved child.

Now there is a chance to end the generations old hate and fear between their clans.

Fate connects them. The desire for peace binds them. Will a rival tear them apart?

Highland Solution

Laird Niall MacIan needs Lady Katherine Ruthven's dowry to relieve his clan's crushing debt but he has no intention of giving her his heart in the bargain.

Niall MacIan, a Highland laird, desperately needs funds to save his impoverished clan. Lady Katherine Ruthven, a lowland heiress, is rumored to be "unmarriageable" and her uncle hopes to be granted her title and lands when the king sends her to a convent.

King David II anxious to strengthen his alliances sees a solution that will give Ruthven the title he wants, and

MacIan the money he needs. Laird MacIan will receive Lady Katherine's hand along with her substantial dowry and her uncle will receive her lands and title.

Lady Katherine must forfeit everything in exchange for a husband who does not want to be married and believes all women to be self-centered and deceitful.

Can the lovely and gentle Katherine mend his heart and build a life with him or will he allow the treachery of others to destroy them?

Highland Courage

Her parents want a betrothal, but Mairead MacKenzie can't get married without revealing her secret and no man will wed her once he knows.

Plain in comparison to her siblings and extremely reserved, Mairead has been called "MacKenzie's Mouse" since she was a child. No one knows the reason for her timidity and she would just as soon keep it that way. When her parents arrange a betrothal to Laird Tadhg Matheson she is horrified. She only sees one way to prevent an old secret from becoming a new scandal.

Tadhg Matheson admires and respects the MacKenzies. While an alliance with them through marriage to Mairead would be in his clan's best interest, he knows Laird MacKenzie seeks a closer alliance with another clan. When Tadhg learns of her terrible shyness and her youngest brother's fears about her, Tadhg offers for her anyway.

Secrets always have a way of revealing themselves. With Tadhg's unconditional love, can Mairead find the strength and courage she needs to handle the consequences when they do?

Highland Intrigue

Lady Gillian MacLennan's clan needs a leader, but the last person on earth she wants as their laird is Fingal MacIan.

She can neither forgive nor forget that his mother killed her father, and, by doing so, created Clan MacLennan's current desperate circumstances.

King David knows a weak clan, without a laird, can change quickly from a simple annoyance to a dangerous liability, and he cannot ignore the turmoil. The MacIan's owe him a great debt, so when he makes Fingal MacIan laird of clan MacLennan and requires that he marry Lady Gillian, Fingal is in no position to refuse.

In spite of the challenge, Fingal is confident he can rebuild her clan, ease her heartache and win her affection. However, just as love awakens, the power struggle takes a deadly turn. Can he protect her from the unknown long enough to uncover the plot against them? Or will all be lost, destroying the happiness they seek in each other's arms?

MJ Platt

Somewhere Montana

Can Callum "Mac" Maclain make Sage Burnett believe in his love for her and save her from her stalker?

Escaping from a stalker, Sage Burnett crashes her plane on a mountain, part of the ranch owned by the man who rejected her eight years ago. She still loves him and prays he isn't around because she dreads facing him to only have him reject her again.

Callum "Mac" MacLain, the ranch owner, a Marine home on medical leave rescues her from the mountain. He persuades her to stay until she heals. He realizes he is still in love with her. Can he save her from her stalker and convince her his love is real?